Bunter Does His Best

Bunter
Does His Best

Frank Richards

Edited by Kay King and
illustrated by Victor Ambrus

QUILLER PRESS
LONDON

Quiller Press Ltd,
11a Albemarle Street,
London W.1.

First published original edition 1954; this edition 1982

ISBN 0 907621 08 2

Production in association with
Book Production Consultants,
Cambridge

Printed in England by
The Burlington Press (Cambridge) Ltd.,
Station Road, Foxton, Cambridge

Contents

Chapter 1

Tribulations of a Football Captain

'You're a clot!' Harry Wharton said to Bob Cherry.

'Thanks!'

'And an idiot!'

'Blow your top if it makes you feel better,' said Bob Cherry, looking down at his badly bruised knee.

Harry scowled. 'You ought to have kept out of the way of that clodhopper.'

'It wasn't Bob's fault,' said Frank Nugent, mildly. 'He didn't ask Bolsover to hack him like that.'

'Br—r—r!' Harry went on nibbling his pencil and staring at a piece of paper. He was the captain of the Remove soccer team, and he already had problems. Now, it seemed, he had another. It looked as if he was going to lose his sweeper.

As he lifted his pencil to cross Bob's name off the team list, he glanced across at him.

'Do you think you can turn out?' he asked.

Ruefully, Bob shook his head. 'Not a hope. See for yourself. I couldn't play marbles, let alone soccer.'

'Br—r—r!'

'I should be all right for the Rookwood game——'

'A fat lot of use that is.' Harry drew a line through Bob's name. 'That's really put the fat in the fire. The team's a mess already. There's Browney coughing and spluttering all over the place, and Linley at home for the weekend—that's two of the midfield players gone. Penfold's out as well. You shouldn't have shoved your knee in front of his boot.'

'Thoughtless of me,' said Bob, with a faint smile.

'It's a thundering nuisance! I'll have to reorganise the team. You'll have to play midfield, Frank. You're nothing like as good as Browney, but I can't see what else I can do.'

'Thanks very much,' said Frank. 'There's nothing like a spot of encouragement to get the best out of someone.'

'There's no need to take it like that!' snapped Harry. 'You know you're not a patch on him.'

'Take it easy, my dear Harry,' murmured Hurree Jamset Ram Singh. 'There is no point in getting wound up.'

'Who's wound up?' demanded Harry, throwing his pencil down.

The Remove team was to play the Courtfield village juniors on Wednesday, and they were a tough side with some very talented players. The Remove had been beaten the last time that they had met, and they were keen to get their revenge. Harry had thought that they had had a good chance of pulling it off, but his team had been plagued by injuries.

Bob, who was rubbing his knee with some liniment, rubbed a little too hard, and groaned. 'Ouch!' he cried, and winced.

Harry stared at him across the table. 'Eh? What's up?' he asked blankly.

'Wow! My knee—' gasped Bob. 'Oh, crikey!'

'Oh! Sorry, Bob. I wasn't thinking about you. I was concentrating on the team. Does it hurt much?'

'Wow!' mumbled Bob again, and went on rubbing, a little more cautiously this time. He groaned. 'It'll be dot and carry one for me for the rest of the week. It's just my luck to have it happen before a match.'

'Courtfield's a strong side,' said Harry, thoughtfully.

'And now I've let you down.'

'Of course you haven't,' said Harry, trying to cheer Bob up. 'Forget it. We'll be weak in midfield, but the defence isn't bad, and we've got Johnny in goal. As for Frank, well, he's nearly as good as Browney.' He caught sight of Frank's face. 'What are you grinning at?' he demanded.

'Oh, nothing,' said Frank, airily.

'There'll be Smithy and Hurree and me up front,' Harry went on. 'That doesn't sound too bad, does it?'

'Smithy's really good,' said Johnny, 'and on his day he can be brilliant. We ought to run Courtfield off their feet.'

'And all I can do is to stand on the sidelines, watching you score,' said Bob.

Harry laughed. 'We'll get the goals, all right. Now, who can I put in to replace you, Bob? Suppose——'

He was interrupted by a fat squeak. 'I say, you fellows.' A fat face and a pair of big spectacles blinked in at the half-open door, and five pairs of eyes glared back. It was impossible to have a serious discussion with Billy Bunter around.

'Hook it, Bunter,' said Harry, briefly.

'Oh, really, Wharton——'

'Buzz off, bread basket!'

'But—but I just happened to hear what you were saying, old chap. You're in a spot of bother, aren't you? If you need a good man for the team, I can tell you where to find one.'

'Oh, yes? Out with it! I'm always ready to listen to advice. Who is it?'

'Me!' said the fat Owl, simply.

There was a stunned silence, followed by a howl of laughter.

'And where would you like to play, my dear dustbin?' asked Hurree Singh. 'Backstop, or silly mid off?'

'Huh! You can't pull my leg,' said Bunter, disdainfully. 'I'm not talking about tennis. I'm on about soccer. I'm a talented striker all right, but I'm jolly useful in midfield. Come to that, I'm a pretty good sweeper—better than Cherry. It's a bit of luck that he's laid up. It'll give you a chance to play a superstar.'

'You?' asked Frank.

'Me!' repeated Bunter, and blinked indignantly as the Famous Five laughed again.

'Joke's over, fat man,' said Harry, grabbing a cushion. 'Beat it!'

'Beast!'

Once the Owl had gone, Harry picked up the list and studied it again. 'No one is as good as you, Bob,' he said. 'There's Redwing. He's keen enough. Smithy will be pleased if I put him in the team. Now, let's see—' There was a tap at the door, and he groaned. 'Don't tell me it's that fat freak again.'

As the door opened, he stared round. 'What are you barging in here for?' he shouted. 'You can—' He broke off. It wasn't Bunter. It was Vernon-Smith who walked in.

'That's what I like,' said Smithy. 'A warm welcome.'

'Sorry. I thought you were that fat porcupine again. I'm glad you've dropped in. I wanted to have a word with you.'

Smithy leaned against the window sill, his hands in his pockets. Although he must have come for some reason, he didn't seem to be in a hurry to begin. In fact, he seemed slightly embarrassed.

The Bounder wasn't always welcome in study no 1. His ways weren't those of the Famous Five. Breaking bounds at night, smoking and gambling didn't appeal to them, and they didn't care for his habit of bending the truth when it suited him, but they were pleased to see him now.

'Take a pew,' said Harry, hospitably.

Smithy remained standing. 'I want to have a word about the Courtfield match,' he said, a trifle awkwardly.

'That's what we've been on about,' said Bob. 'If I'd got two good legs instead of one, I'd boot Bolsover all over the school.'

'It's rotten luck,' said Smithy.

'You're telling me,' agreed Harry. 'What a headache. I've lost four of my best players. I was thinking of playing Redwing. What do you think?'

'Where?'

'He'll have to replace Bob.'

The Bounder hesitated. 'He's a better striker,' he said, at last.

'I don't have a problem with strikers.'

'But you do,' said Smithy quietly.

Harry looked puzzled. 'I don't know what you mean.' He picked up his pencil, and added Redwing's name to the list. 'There you are.'

'Hang on,' said Smithy, quickly.

'What for?'

'Well——'

'Well what?'

Smithy took a deep breath. 'I'm not playing on Wednesday.'

'What?' Harry dropped his pencil.

'Sorry.'

'What's wrong with you?' demanded Harry.

'Nothing.'

'Then why can't you play?'

The Bounder flushed. 'I've got something else on.'

'What is it?'

'It doesn't matter what it is. I'm giving you fair warning.'

Harry leaned his elbows on the table, and stared at Smithy. 'Why aren't you going to turn out?'

The Bounder looked sullen. 'That's my business. It's not as if it's an important game.'

'They're all important,' growled Johnny.

Smithy shrugged. 'Well, I can't play.'

'You mean that you won't play,' said Harry Wharton, looking hard at him.

'You can put it that way if you like.' Smithy turned to leave.

'Hold on,' said Harry, quietly. 'This isn't the end of

the matter.' His eyes were cold as he looked at the Bounder.

'It's no good. I've made up my mind.'

'You'd better listen, Smithy. I can guess what's more important than the game.' Harry's voice was scornful. 'You're going to the races or playing billiards or something like that, and I bet you're joining forces with Ponsonby and his rotten crowd from Courtfield School.'

'Think what you like.'

Harry leaned forward. 'Listen. We've lost four of the team already. If you leave us in the lurch, we won't stand a dog's chance. I expect you to turn out, Smithy.'

The Bounder's eyes narrowed. 'I shall be miles away on Wednesday. Take my name off the list.'

'But you can't mean it, my dear Smithy,' exclaimed Hurree, in dismay.

'But I do.'

'You're a louse,' said Bob, flatly.

'If you think so.'

'Well, I can't make you—' said Harry.

'That's right.'

'And you want to be crossed off the list?'

'It's sunk in at last, has it?' said the Bounder, sarcastically.

'Okay, if that's what you want, I'll do it, but it won't appear on any other list this season, Smithy, and that's flat. We'd never know if we could count on you. Something else a bit more interesting might crop up. Think it over before I draw a line through your name.'

The Bounder's eyes glittered. 'Are you threatening me, Wharton?'

'No. I'm warning you.'

'Don't be a fool, Smithy. Ponsonby and his mob aren't worth it,' said Bob.

'Well?' Harry sat erect, his pencil poised.

The Bounder gave him a black look. 'I've told you. I'm not playing, and that's my last word. If you think you can keep me out of the team for ever, then you've got another think coming,' and he marched out of the study, slamming the door behind him.

'Right,' said Harry, and drew a line through Smithy's name. 'That's that!'

Chapter 2

Six for Smithy

'I say, you fellows!'

'Get out!' yelled the Bounder.

It wasn't Billy Bunter's day. Half an hour ago, he hadn't been wanted in study no 1. Now, it seemed, he was wanted even less in study no 4. The look that Smithy shot at him as he blinked in the doorway was almost deadly.

Outbursts of rage were not uncommon in that study. When Smithy was in a vile temper, he simply let rip. Tom Redwing, the Bounder's study-mate, was a quiet and good-natured chap, and other members of the Remove wondered how he could put up with it when Smithy was ranting away, but he did. In fact, although they were quite different, they were good friends.

Smithy was in a filthy mood because his conscience was nudging him. Although he felt badly about letting Wharton down, he was still going to please himself. He had felt angry when he had left study no 1, and he became even angrier when Redwing said that he was behaving like a rat.

As the Owl opened the study door, Redwing said, 'It's rotten. You ought to be ashamed of yourself.'

'Oh, I say, that's telling him, Reddy!' squeaked Bunter.

'Get out, you tattling toad!' shouted Smithy.

'But I say—I—I haven't come to tea, if that's what you think. I came to say—Yaroooh!'

Bunter broke off with a frantic yell as a heavy Latin dictionary whizzed across the room and landed with a thud on the fattest chin in Greyfriars. The Owl tottered backwards, and fell with a heavy thud.

'Yaroooo! Ow, wow! Beast!'

Vernon-Smith got up and kicked the door shut, and sat down again, his scowl deepening as he saw contemptuous disapproval on Redwing's face. 'You didn't want that fat guzzler to tea, did you?'

'No, but there was no need to blast him like that. He might have come for something else. You didn't give him a chance.'

'Rot! He was scrounging!'

'But Smithy——'

'That fat fiend's always butting in!'

Redwing went back to their previous discussion. 'About Wednesday, Smithy. You can't let the team down. It's——'

He was interrupted by a howl through the keyhole. 'Yah! Beast! Rotter! I'm jolly well not going to tell you that Quelch sent me to say that he wants your lines, so there! Yah!'

'See,' said Redwing, with quiet satisfaction. 'He did come here for something. You shouldn't have chucked that dictionary at him.'

'Shut up!'

'Have you done those lines for Quelch?'

'No, I haven't. I've had other things on my mind. Quelch can drop dead. I'm fed up with him. Come to that, I'm fed up with you, too. It isn't a crime to drop out of a soccer match, is it?'

Redwing looked steadily at Smithy. 'If you were a sport, you wouldn't do it.'

'So I'm not a sport!' Smithy looked even angrier.

'You're not behaving like one. Wharton had lost

. . . A HEAVY LATIN DICTIONARY WHIZZED ACROSS THE
ROOM AND LANDED WITH A THUD . . .

three out of the team even before Cherry was injured, and now you're making it worse just because you're off with Ponsonby's gang, and you know what I think about them!'

'You can think what you like.'

'They're a bunch of rotters. They only care about themselves. They don't give two hoots for anyone else. They're the dregs of Courtfield.'

'So what?' sneered the Bounder.

'The whole form will be up in arms if you clear off,' warned Redwing.

The Bounder shrugged. 'As if I care.'

'You're as bad as Ponsonby.'

'So you think that I'm a rotter as well as a bad sport? Maybe you'd better leave it at that before I do you an injury.'

Redwing tried again. 'Think again. Go to Wharton——'

'You've got a hope!' Smithy pulled open the table drawer and fished out a cigarette and matches. Staring defiantly at Redwing, he lit up. He knew that Redwing hated to see him smoking and he seldom did it while his friend was there, but now he blew a cloud of smoke towards him.

'Put it out!' Reddy said, sharply.

'Clear out if you don't like it.'

'I will.'

As Redwing got up, the Bounder deliberately blew another stream of smoke in his direction. At the same moment, there was a sharp tap on the door, and it was pushed open.

'Hell's bells!' gasped Smithy, as the tall, angular figure of Mr Quelch, his form master, appeared.

'Vernon-Smith, I asked Bunter——'

Hastily, the Bounder whipped the cigarette from his mouth, but he was too late. There was the glowing cigarette, a spiral of smoke rising in the air. He stubbed it out, and got to his feet, his face red.

Quelch's face was furious. 'Vernon-Smith! How dare you smoke! I gave you a hundred lines only last Friday when I caught you at it. I was far too lenient. I shall not make the same mistake again. Go to my study immediately. I shall deal with you there.'

The Bounder walked down the Remove passage, his face sullen.

'Give me the rest of the cigarettes, Redwing,' said Quelch, and then he followed Smithy down the passage.

Once in his study, he didn't waste time. 'You have broken one of the strictest rules in the school,' he said grimly. 'I shall cane you, Vernon-Smith,' and he did.

The Bounder didn't make a sound, but he was pale-faced at the end of his punishment.

'I will not permit you to smoke here! I shall take a very serious view of the matter if I catch you at it again. And now, you wretched boy, fetch me your lines.'

'I—I haven't done them,' muttered the Bounder.

'Indeed?' Quelch raised his eyebrows. 'Then I shall double them. You will bring me two hundred lines before prep. If you do not, I shall send you to the head-master, and let Dr Locke deal with you. That is all.'

Silently, the Bounder left Quelch's study, and walked down the master's corridor.

Redwing was waiting for him. He looked at the Bounder's pale face. 'Hard luck, Smithy.'

'I'll get my own back!' said the Bounder, venom-ously. 'He really piled it on, but he won't get away with it. I swear he won't. He even doubled my lines.'

'I'll give you hand with them.'

'Don't be such a fool!' snapped Smithy. 'He'd spot it straight away. Anyway, I can do without your help.'

'Please yourself,' said Redwing quietly, and he walked away. It was clear that the Bounder wanted to pick a quarrel with someone, and he didn't care who it was. It could be friend or foe. In his present black

'I WILL NOT PERMIT YOU TO SMOKE HERE!'

mood, it made no difference who it was.

Smithy made his way back to his study and walked restlessly up and down. He knew that he had to settle down and write those lines, but first he had to wait for the effect of Quelch's punishment to wear off.

The door opened, and Skinner poked his head round it. 'Smithy,' he began.

'Get out, Skinner!' snapped the Bounder.

'I only wanted to tell you that Wharton put up the soccer team in the Rag. He's left you out, and I thought you'd like——'

'Clear out! Leave me alone!'

'There's no need to jump down my throat,' said Skinner. 'If Wharton's kicked you out of the team, it isn't my fault, is it?'

'If I wanted to play, I'd play!'

'Oh, yes?' jeered Skinner. 'I thought that Wharton was captain.'

Smithy took one quick stride across the room, and picked up the Latin dictionary again. 'I'll slam you on the head if you don't get out,' he snarled.

'Okay, okay,' said Skinner quickly, as he backed out.

Scowling, Smithy got out paper, pen and ink, and reluctantly started to write. He was still fuming, and bitterly resentful. Somehow or other, he was going to get his own back on Quelch.

Chapter 3

Billy Bunter's Booby-trap

'Hallo, hallo, hallo! What's your game?'

'Oh!' gasped the fat Owl, startled, and he gave Bob Cherry a nervous blink.

Up to that moment, Billy Bunter had thought that he was alone in the Remove passage. The bell had not yet rung for prep and practically everyone was in the

Rag, talking about soccer. He hadn't known that Bob had come upstairs to give his damaged knee another rub with linament.

'What are you doing there?' Bob asked, eyeing Bunter, who was standing outside the half-open door of study no 4, a large bag clasped to his fat chest.

'Eh? What? What do you mean? I—I ain't up to anything. I'm not standing by Smithy's door. This—this ain't a bag of flour. I—I say, Bob, old man, did you know Smithy's not in the team? They're all talking about it in the Rag—happened to hear Squiff say he—he wanted your opinion. Perhaps you'd better go and give it.'

'Whatever it is that you're thinking of doing, you fat chump,' said Bob, 'you'd better think again. Smithy's had a bit of trouble with Quelch, and I think he's feeling pretty sore about it.'

'Got whacked did he?'

'That's right. He's in a vile temper.'

'Fat lot I care,' said Bunter, disdainfully. 'I'm not afraid of Smithy. We Bunters don't take insults lightly. Do you know, he chucked a dictionary at me? Got me right on the chin. Well, it's my turn now.'

'Where did that bag of flour come from?'

'Flour? Did I say flour? Well, it ain't, and I didn't get it from the kitchen neither. If Mrs Kebble says she's lost a bag of flour, don't you go saying anything about it. I don't want her thinking it was me.'

'If I were you,' advised Bob, 'I'd take it back, and forget about Smithy.'

'Not likely,' said the Owl. 'Tee, hee, hee!' His fat shoulders heaved. 'Smithy won't half be mad when it lands on top of his nut. Tee, hee, hee!'

'It won't be so funny when he gets hold of you,' warned Bob.

'He won't know it was me,' said Bunter confidently. 'I—I say, Bob, old man, lend me a hand, will you? I can't reach the top of the door, but you can. I want it balanced up there so that it'll crash on top of Smithy when he opens the door.'

'It might land on top of Redwing.'

'Eh?' Bunter looked downcast. 'But it's got to be Smithy. I'll tell you what. You go down to the Rag and keep Redwing talking. Say something interesting.' He wrinkled his fat brow. 'I've got it. His father's in the navy, isn't he? Well, you can tell him that his boat's gone down with all hands lost——'

'You crazy cuckoo!' shouted Bob.

Bunter stared. He thought it a good idea, but he could see it hadn't gone down well. 'And—and then you can tell him later on that it was only a joke.'

'You fat porpoise! I'd jolly well boot you along the passage if I could.'

'Beast!'

'Now look here, fat man. Don't do it. Smithy will skin you alive if he gets caught in that booby-trap.'

'Yah! If you haven't got the nerve, I'll do it myself, and I'll jolly well make sure it's Smithy who gets smothered in flour. I ain't going to waste it on Redwing. You mind your own business, Bob Cherry —no, no, I didn't mean that, old man. Come on. Be a sport. Balance the bag on the top of the door for me.'

'You're asking for trouble, Bunter, but it's your funeral,' said Bob, and he limped off down the passage.

'Beast!' snorted Bunter.

He blinked up at the door. He wasn't tall enough to reach the top, and so he bowled off to his own study, and returned with a chair. Laboriously, he clambered onto it, the bag of flour still firmly clasped in his arms, but as he lifted the flour it touched the top of the door so that it swung open, out of his reach.

'Blow!' he muttered. He blinked down the passage. Time was ticking past, and he was anxious to set the trap and clear off before anyone came up for prep. He climbed down again, stepped into Smithy's study, and grasped the door handle, but then he froze as he heard

. . . AS HE LIFTED THE FLOUR . . .

footsteps and voices, coming along the passage.

'Oh, crikey!' It was the Bounder's voice. He stood there, rooted to the spot, the bag still in his arms.

'Stop nagging, Redwing! I've had enough from the chaps in the Rag without listening to you wittering on.'

'Well, what did you expect? You've let them down.'

'Belt up! I don't want to hear any more about it.' There was a crash. 'What's this chair doing here?' Smithy kicked it again. He flung open the door, and saw Bunter. 'What are you doing here?' he demanded. 'What—?' He stopped, seeing the bag of flour in the Owl's fat paws.

'Nun—nun—nothing. I ain't doing nothing,' stammered the Owl.

'Oh, no? You—you fat fiend! You weren't thinking of setting a booby-trap, were you?'

'No—no!' squeaked the Owl hastily. Smithy looked dangerous. 'No, I wouldn't do that to you, Smithy. Not me. I—I thought I'd—I'd—' He looked at the flour, and inspiration came. 'I—I thought I'd make a cake for you, Smithy, old man.'

'Did you?'

'Just thought you'd—you'd like a surprise——'

'Really?' Smithy doubled his fists.

'You're a prize clot, Bunter,' said Redwing. He grinned at Smithy. 'Let him push off. He hasn't done any harm.'

Smithy looked at the Owl. 'Give me the bag of flour,' he said

'Oh, certainly, old man. But, if—if——'

The Bounder snatched the flour. 'I think I'll make the same sort of cake that you were planning for me.'

'Oh, gum drops! Oh—er——'

'Hang on to him, Redwing!' snapped the Bounder. 'Hold him while I burst the bag——'

'Yaroooo!' shouted the Owl. He bounded towards the door.

'Grab him!' shouted Smithy, but Redwing stepped aside so that Owl was able to escape. 'You fool, Redwing! Why didn't you stop him?'

'For goodness sake, Smithy!' said Redwing. 'Leave him alone.'

Vernon-Smith gave his friend a savage look. He banged the flour on the table. 'And yet you say that you're a friend of mine,' he said, bitterly. 'You know that he meant it for me. I dare say you'd have enjoyed seeing me covered in flour.'

'Don't be so stupid. Anyway, you know why Bunter was doing it. You hit him with that dictionary for no reason. Why don't you try to control your temper?'

'Are you looking for a row?' demanded Smithy.

'Oh, dry up! You make me tired!'

Smithy looked at Redwing in astonishment. He had never spoken to him like that before. 'What's got into you?'

Redwing took no notice, but sorted out his books for prep, and then he looked at the flour. 'We'll have to get rid of that,' he said. 'We'll nip down to the kitchen when the coast is clear. We don't want to be caught with it.'

'Don't bother,' said the Bounder, quickly. He picked it up, and stowed it in the cupboard. 'I'll deal with it later on.'

'Oh?' Redwing gave him a keen look.

Smithy gave a little smile. 'I'm glad I didn't burst it over Bunter after all,' he said. 'I can think of another use for it. I've got a little score to settle.'

Redwing looked puzzled at first, and then he gasped. 'Smithy!' he exclaimed. 'Don't tell me that you're thinking of Quelch. You must be off your rocker. You wouldn't dare!'

'Wouldn't I?' Smithy gave a harsh laugh.

'But——'

'Oh, dry up. You make me tired,' said the Bounder, mockingly.

Chapter 4

Unpopular!

Billy Bunter stood in the sunshine the following morning. He was leaning in front of the tuckshop, his plump hands in the pockets of the tightest trousers in Greyfriars. There was a grin on his face in spite of the fact that he hadn't had the best of mornings.

Quelch had already given him a hundred lines for not having done his prep, his long-awaited postal order hadn't arrived, and he was outside Mrs Mimble's instead of inside where he longed to be.

It was the sight of Vernon-Smith coming out of the tuckshop that made him smile. The Bounder, confident as ever, closed the door, and then looked up in surprise at a small knot of grim-faced fellows who closed in on him.

'Get out of the way!' he snapped, irritably.

'No!' said Quincy Iffley Field. 'Not until we've had a word with you.'

'I can't think of anything I want to say to you, Squiff.'

'You're letting the team down, Smithy.'

'Too bad,' drawled the Bounder. 'Well, now you've said it, get out of the way.'

'Not yet,' Peter Todd said. 'We haven't finished yet.'

'But I have.' The Bounder tried to elbow his way through the group.

'You're a rotten sport,' said Russell. 'You know how much you're needed for the match. You're letting everyone down.'

'You jolly well know that Wharton's lost four men,' Squiff said. 'The village team will have a walkover if you drop out.'

'We won't stand an earthly,' added Russell.

The Bounder didn't answer, but he scowled at them. He had been badgered by members of the team ever since the list had gone up, and he was aware that his popularity was at its lowest ebb. He didn't like it, but he wasn't going to do anything about it.

'Change your mind,' urged Squiff.

'I can't. I've got something else fixed up.'

'What?' demanded Peter Todd.

Smithy fell silent again.

'Well?' asked Russell.

There was a fat chuckle. 'Hee, hee, hee!' sniggered Billy Bunter. 'Hee, hee, hee! I know what it is. He's going out with that rotter Ponsonby. They're going to the races. Heard him telling Skinner. Hee, hee, hee!'

'What!' burst out Ogilvy.

The Bounder threw an angry look at the fat Owl. His eyes glittered, and he made for him, but the juniors blocked his way.

'Is that what you're chucking us over for?' demanded Russell. 'If it is, you really are a worm.'

'It's none of your business!' rapped the Bounder.

Squiff gave him a hard look. 'It is our business.'

'And you think that going to the races is more important than turning out for the team?' demanded Toddy. 'If that's it, you're the dregs.'

'Let me pass!'

'Not yet,' said Squiff, firmly. 'We're offering you a last chance, Smithy. Go to Wharton and say that you'll play.'

'But I won't.'

'And that's final?'

'Yes.'

'Right! That's it!' said Squiff. 'Collar him!'

The Bounder's eyes blazed, and he made a determined attempt to break through the ring of juniors surrounding him, but hands shot out, grabbed him roughly, and hustled him towards the fountain.

'Let go!' he snarled. 'Let go before I——'

'Duck him!' shouted Squiff.

'Shove his head under water!' yelled Russell.

There was a splash, and water shot into the air as Smithy's head was thrust into the water, and pushed down.

'Tee, hee, hee! That's right!' squeaked Billy Bunter. 'Go on. Do it again. That'll learn him to chuck dictionaries about. Serve him jolly well right.'

Vernon-Smith was ducked again and again. 'That'll do,' said Squiff.

The Bounder stood upright, with water running down his neck and soaking his shirt, and he glared with speechless fury at the small crowd.

'You can clear off,' said Squiff, 'now we've shown you what we think of you.'

'Yes,' added Toddy. 'Clear off before you get kicked off.'

The Bounder swung round, and his eyes narrowed. Then, choked with rage, he tramped off towards the school.

As he squelched his way towards the entrance, he ran into the Famous Five. Four of them grinned at the dripping Bounder, but Harry Wharton gave him a cold, contemptuous glance, and passed on.

Smithy grabbed at his sleeve. 'You're behind this, aren't you, Wharton?' he said, thickly. 'You set that pack of jackasses on me. If you think you can make me change my mind, you've got another think coming.'

Harry shook off the Bounder's hand. 'You are quite, quite wrong,' he said coolly. 'I'm not interested in whether you change your mind or not. You're out, and you're staying out,' and he walked on.

'I'd go in and find a towel, if I were you,' said Bob Cherry, grinning at Vernon-Smith. 'You look a bit of a drip.'

The Bounder flung him a furious look. He was just about to step inside when Wingate, the captain of the school, caught sight of him. 'What have you been up to, Vernon-Smith?' he demanded. 'You're soaking. What's been going on?'

'Oh, nothing,' muttered the Bounder. He didn't want to admit that he had been ducked and, to give him his due, he didn't want to split on anyone. 'We—we were messing about. It was an accident.'

'Oh, yes?' said Wingate, eyeing him doubtfully. He hesitated a moment, and then decided to let it go. 'All right, get inside and dry yourself off, you silly fool, but you'd better not have another accident like that.'

Smithy stamped his way towards the lobby, and ran into Skinner who had witnessed the scene from a safe distance. There were times when Smithy and Skinner were quite thick, but there was a malicious streak in Skinner, and he was quite pleased to see the Bounder being ragged.

'You look a bit wet, Smithy,' he sneered, and then made the mistake of making the same joke as Bob Cherry. 'You look a bit of a drip.'

The Bounder gave him a furious look, and then pushed him so hard that he went sprawling. 'Shut up!' Smithy marched into the cloakroom and grabbed a towel. Almost bursting with fury, he ripped off his tie and shirt, and began to rub himself down.

'Smithy!' exclaimed Redwing, rushing in. 'What's happened? What's been going on? I met that idiot Bunter, and he said——'

'You've got eyes in your head, haven't you?' snapped the Bounder. 'I've been ducked.'

'But why on earth——?'

'Don't be such a fool!'

'It's because of Wednesday, I suppose.'

'You suppose right,' muttered Smithy, as he stood there rubbing at his wet hair.

'I'm sorry, Smithy,' said Redwing, 'but I'm not surprised. The chaps have been——'

'Oh, shut up! The last thing I need is a lecture from you!' said Smithy, glowering at Redwing.

Redwing's sympathy began to run out. 'You asked for it,' he said. 'You've let everyone down, you know that you have. They're sick of you, and sick of your rotten, selfish behaviour. You think that you can do just what you like and get away with it. Well, just for once you haven't. Maybe it'll teach you that you can't trample over people.'

Angrily, the Bounder stood in front of Redwing, his fists clenched. There was a sullen look on his face. 'Just you listen to me, Redwing——' he began.

'The last thing that I want to do is to listen to you,' Redwing replied, and giving the Bounder a cold look, he turned and walked silently from the cloakroom.

Vernon-Smith was left feeling resentful and depressed. If Redwing turned against him, he would be left without a friend.

Chapter 5

Smithy Thinks Twice

Bob Cherry limped into the Rag. His friends were outside, punting a ball about, but since he couldn't join in, he'd decided not to hang around. He wasn't looking forward to being a spectator instead of a player on the following day, and so he was gloomy-faced as he made his way into the common room.

His face became even gloomier as he saw Smithy sitting at a table, a pen in his hand, and a sheet of paper and an envelope in front of him. If Bob's knee hadn't been hurting so much, he'd have been tempted to kick the Bounder.

There were several other members of the Remove in the Rag, and they were all watching Smithy. Redwing looked unhappy, but the others were looking scornful. The Bounder appeared to be unaware of them. His elbow was on the table, and his chin was cupped in his hand, and he had a thoughtful expression on his face. He hadn't got very far with his letter. Up to now, as several juniors had noticed, he had only written "Dear Ponsonby".

Bob thought it odd that Smithy was writing so openly to him. Although the Bounder seldom cared what people thought of him, his unpopularity was so great that it must have stung his pride, and yet he was risking even more trouble by letting people see he was writing to Ponsonby.

Vernon-Smith glanced at Bob as he hobbled over to a chair. 'Knee still bad?' he asked.

'It's just as well that it is,' said Bob, grimly. 'It's itching to kick you round the quad. I'm jolly glad that they ducked your cheeky head. It made me feel a bit better.'

The Bounder gave a quiet laugh. 'Thanks. Shall I send your kind regards to Ponsonby?' he asked blandly.

'You're writing to that rat, are you?'

'That's right.'

'About your little trip tomorrow, I suppose.'

'Right again.'

Bob looked around the common room. 'Pity about my knee,' he said. 'Anyone willing to do the job for me? What about you, Squiff?'

Squiff advanced towards the table. 'Pleasure,' he said, and several other chaps followed him.

Tom Redwing looked up sharply, and made a movement as if to stand by his friend, but he checked it. If Smithy was determined to ask for trouble, that was his business.

The Bounder didn't seem at all alarmed. On the contrary, he smiled.

'Grab him!' said Bolsover.

'Boot him!' shouted Ogilvy.

Vernon-Smith waved the letter in the air. 'Hang on,' he said. 'Let me finish this. I want to catch the next post so that Ponsonby will get it first thing tomorrow morning.'

'Tee, hee, hee!' tittered Bunter. 'Lucky Quelch doesn't know what he's going to be up to tomorrow afternoon. He told Skinner——'

'I'm going to stuff that letter down your neck, Smithy, and then I'll boot you round the room!' shouted Squiff.

'Okay,' said Smithy. 'I can't stop you, but it seems a pity when I'm letting him know that I'm cancelling my jaunt. I'm telling him that I'll be playing soccer instead.'

'Oh!'

'What?'

'Honestly?'

'Smithy!' exclaimed Redwing, with relief, his face brightening. 'That's great!' He walked over to the table. 'I knew you'd change your mind. I felt sure you would. I—I knew you couldn't let us all down.'

The Bounder gave another quiet laugh. 'I didn't have much option, did I? It was all the lectures you gave me that did it——'

'Oh, come on,' said Redwing.

'Those, and a ducking. It's amazing what effect they had. I'm glad you bothered.'

Most of the juniors eyed Smithy doubtfully. His change of heart had happened surprisingly quickly, but maybe he'd realised that he'd gone too far.

'You really mean it?' asked Bob.

'I usually mean what I say.'

'And you are going to play?'

'You've got it in one.'

'You're not having us on?' asked Toddy.

'Of course he isn't!' Redwing leapt to his friend's defence.

'Well, let's see what you're going to write,' said Toddy, suspiciously.

'All right,' said Smithy. 'You can read it when I've

finished, and you can post it yourself.'

'Fine.'

Smithy scribbled a rapid note, and then he handed it to Toddy while he addressed the envelope.

Toddy smiled, and passed it on to Squiff. 'That's all right,' he said.

'Good-oh!' Squiff said. 'Good for you, Smithy.'

Skinner read it. 'Very cunning. Not a word about the races,' he said. 'You're just cancelling the outing.'

'Do you think that I'm mad? It could get into the wrong hands. I wouldn't want old Pon to get into trouble because of me.' He handed over the envelope to Toddy. 'You'll have to get a stamp,' he said. 'I haven't got one down here.'

'It'll be a pleasure,' said Toddy, stuffing the letter into the envelope. 'I'll nip off to the postbox straight away. I shan't be long.'

Bob gave the Bounder a hearty smack on the shoulders. 'That's terrific!' he said.

'Ouch! Take it easy. You'll put me on the sick list if you don't watch out.'

There was a burst of laughter as the Bounder got up, his popularity restored.

'Where are you going?' asked Redwing.

'To find Wharton, of course. I've got to let him know.'

Several chaps followed him.

'He's still outside, I think,' said Bob, as they went down the passage. A few minutes later they ran into Harry and Frank who had just come in.

'Wharton!' said the Bounder.

'Yes?' said Harry, coldly. 'What is it?'

'About the match tomorrow——'

Harry cut him short. 'There's nothing to say. The list is up. Redwing's playing.'

'I thought you might like to know that I can turn out tomorrow after all.'

The little crowd looked eagerly at Harry, expecting

him to look as delighted as they felt. His expression didn't alter. 'You're playing tomorrow?'

'Yep.'

'You do mean soccer?'

'Of course I do,' said the Bounder, sharply.

'I just wondered if you had some other sport in mind. Well, if you want a game, I hope you find one. Was there anything else that you wanted to say?'

Smithy's eyes glittered. 'I thought you'd be pleased to know that I've put Ponsonby off.'

'That's good of you,' said Harry, 'but you've wasted your time. I told you that if you decided not to play, it would be the end of soccer for you.'

Bob Cherry looked dismayed. 'Harry—' he began.

'We need Smithy in the team,' said Redwing, quickly.

'Do we?' Harry gave Smithy a hard look. 'Do we really need someone who might let us down again if he felt like it? He's already changed his mind once. Who's to say that he won't do it again?'

'You know that I wouldn't.'

'Do I?' said Harry, coldly. 'I do know that you can't be trusted. I made it perfectly clear that you weren't going to play at all if you opted out when you were needed. I'd sooner put Bunter in the team than you, Vernon-Smith. As long as I'm captain, you're not playing for the Remove.'

'Maybe you won't be games captain much longer,' said the Bounder, vindictively.

Harry shrugged. 'That's for the form to decide. If they don't want me, then I'll step down, but until that happens, there's no place in the team for you.'

The Bounder clenched his fist, tempted to smash it into that cool, contemptuous face. It had never crossed his mind that Harry might not welcome him back into the team. 'You might be sorry for this, Wharton!' he said, angrily.

'Perhaps.'

As Harry turned to walk away, a number of voices were raised in protest.

'Wharton——!'

'You're cutting off your nose to spite your face!'

'We won't stand a chance without Smithy.'

Harry swung round and faced the fellows. 'Listen. Smithy was picked for the team. He dropped out even though he knew what would happen if he did. All right, he's changed his mind, but I haven't. I'm the games captain of the Remove, and I'm not chopping and changing just to suit Smithy.'

'But still—' began Redwing.

'I can't hang about waiting to see if Smithy's going to play or not. You might think that that's the way a captain should carry on, but I don't,' Harry said, scornfully.

'I know, but——'

'There aren't any buts as far as I'm concerned.'

'We want Smithy, and he's willing to play. That's the point, Wharton,' said Toddy.

'His place has been filled,' said Harry, firmly. 'Redwing's playing.'

'He'd give it up for me,' snapped Smithy.

Wharton gave another shrug. 'When Redwing's captain, he can decide who plays where.'

'The village team will have a field day,' said Smithy, and there was a murmur of agreement.

Harry gave him a withering look. 'You've changed your tune, haven't you. You couldn't have cared less yesterday. Anyway the matter's settled. You dropped out, and you're going to stay out,' and he walked away.

Frank and Bob gave each other anxious looks as they followed Harry down the passage. Harry turned to them.

'Do you think I should have given in?'

'Um,' said Bob, uncomfortably. 'We don't want to be beaten twice running.'

'Smithy's maddening,' said Frank. 'But I think he should play—and most of the others will think the same.'

Harry nodded. 'I know, but I think I'm right. I can't give in. If Smithy gets away with this, he'll think he can run the whole show. If the form wants him as captain, they can have him. He can skipper the side for the rest of the season—provided he isn't in detention for smoking or drinking or something, but as long as I'm in charge, he isn't playing.'

Frank and Bob looked at each other. There wasn't anything that they could say. Harry had made his mind up, and he wasn't going to change it for anyone, but they had an uncomfortable feeling that there was trouble brewing.

Chapter 6

Adamant!

Lord Mauleverer strolled into the Rag after class that day, his hands in his pockets, and an unusually thoughtful expression on his face. Instead of making for an armchair as usual, he wandered across to the notice board and stood looking at the soccer list for some time, and then he shook his head.

Mauly was hardly an enthusiast when it came to games, but unlike Snoop, Skinner, Billy Bunter and one or two others, he never tried to dodge them. Had he been asked to play for form, he would have been filled with dismay, but he did do his best to support the team. As long as he was reminded, he turned up on the sidelines and cheered his side on.

The list that he read wasn't very impressive, considering their opponents, and he shook his head again. He strolled across to the window, and joined Harry

Wharton who was staring out into the quad. A crowd of the Remove standing outside, and talking excitedly.

Harry took a deep breath. By now, most people had told him they thought he'd made a mistake and he had no doubt that they were still talking about it.

'Just been looking at the team,' said Mauly.

'Becoming keen on soccer?' asked Harry, lightly.

'Yaas, in a way.' Mauly gave a little cough. 'Mind if I say something?'

'Say what you like,' Harry said, carelessly.

'Don't want to interfere, you know.'

'Carry on. Spit it out, Mauly.'

'Last thing I want to do is to get your back up.'

'You won't.'

'Why not make a concession and play Smithy? Fellow's a pain in the neck at times. Behaved badly, no doubt about that. Once he's in the team again, he'll crow, and go on crowing—that's the sort of fellow he is, but it's the game that matters.' He gave Harry a quick look, and went on, 'Difficult for Redwing, too. He's got Smithy's place, but Smithy's his friend. He'd jump at the chance to give it up to Smithy. Why not stretch a point and write in Smithy's name?'

Wharton shook his head.

'Dare say you're right, but that's not what the chaps think.'

'I know.'

'They want to see the team win.'

Harry gave Mauly a faint smile. 'Thinking that there's going to be trouble over this, are you? Well, thanks for the warning, but I'm not changing my mind.'

'Fair enough,' said Mauly. 'Just thought I'd mention it.'

At that moment, Redwing came into the common room, and he too walked over to the window. Mauly glanced at Redwing's flushed face and troubled eyes. The Bounder, he guessed, was giving Redwing a hard time. Casually, he stolled away, and sat quietly in an armchair, watching Harry and Redwing.

'Look here, Wharton,' Redwing said, awkwardly.

'Yes?' Harry had a good idea of what Redwing was going to say.

'About tomorrow's match——'

'There's nothing to worry about,' said Harry, cheerfully. 'Everything's under control.'

'I know Smithy has behaved badly,' Redwing said, quietly, 'and I've told him so more than once, but now he wants to make up for it. Most of us think he should be given a second chance.'

'Somebody doesn't,' said Harry.

'Oh? Who's that?'

'Me.'

Redwing bit his lip. 'I know how you feel, but you've made your point. Smithy isn't going to let you down again.'

'He won't get a chance,' said Harry, flatly.

Redwing looked miserable. 'The only reason that I'm playing is because Smithy isn't.'

'Actually, it was Smithy who suggested you as a striker.'

'I know, but things are different now. Can't you see that? I know that Smithy needled you, but——'

Harry gave him a cool look. 'That is nothing to do with it. I happen to take the job as captain seriously. Smithy opted out, and I'm not letting him opt in again just because it suits him.'

'But Wharton, hardly anyone is on your side over this. Couldn't you think again?' As Harry remained silent, Redwing went on, 'Smithy's ready and willing to play. He's really keen. I can't replace him, you know I can't. I'm nothing like as good.' He paused again, and then said quickly, 'I'm sorry, Wharton, but if you won't, I'm not playing either. You'll have to find another striker.'

'I thought that was coming,' Harry said. 'I was

pretty sure that Smithy would make things as tough for me as he could.'

'I—I'm sorry,' stammered Redwing.

'You needn't be,' said Harry, calmly. 'I know that Smithy put you up to it. It's a pity that you're letting me down, but it can't be helped. I'll cope somehow.'

Redwing's face went red. 'That's hardly fair. Smithy's available. You ought to select him. Everyone says so.'

'Everyone can say what everyone thinks,' drawled Harry. 'It makes no difference.'

He pulled out a pencil, walked across to the notice board, and crossed out Redwing's name, and he stood there, thinking.

Both Mauly and Redwing eyed him with interest, wondering who he was going to put in. At last, he scribbled a name. As he walked away, they got up to see who the substitute was.

'Oh, gad!' gasped Mauly, thunderstruck.

'You can't mean it!' exclaimed Redwing, astonished.

'Why not?'

'You must be off your head!'

'Thanks!' said Mauly, faintly. 'Nothing like speaking your mind.'

'I can rely on Mauly,' said Harry, firmly. 'At least he won't walk out on me at the last minute. I'm much better off with someone I can trust.' He smiled at his friend. 'You'll have to pull your socks up, Mauly, old man.'

'Oh, gad!' repeated Mauly. 'I'll do my best.'

'I knew I could count on you.' Harry strolled back to the window, looking as if he hadn't a care in the world.

Redwing, now even more troubled than he had been when he had entered the Rag, left the room, unhappily aware that instead of making things better, he had made them worse.

Lord Mauleverer sighed aloud. Although a strenuous game of soccer was not his idea of fun, it didn't occur to him to refuse. He would back Harry up whatever happened, and he could imagine what the Remove would say when they found out that he was in the team.

Harry looked at his watch. 'Tea time,' he said. 'The others are beginning to come in. Going to join us?'

'No thanks.' Mauly shook his head. 'I'm already booked.'

By the time that Harry reached study no 1, his friends were already there. Although they looked rather down in the mouth, Harry retained his rather remote but cheerful air. It wasn't long before the talk turned to the team again.

'If we don't win, it'll rebound on you,' warned Bob.

'Too bad.'

'You're riding for a fall,' grunted Johnny Bull.

'Storing up trouble,' remarked Frank.

'I think you are unwise,' said Hurree Singh.

The door opened, and a fat face appeared. 'I say, you chaps——'

'Ring off, Bunter!' said Frank, wearily.

'Shan't! Only came to have a word. I heard you all going on at Wharton. You're rotten. You ought to back him up.'

'What's that?' grunted Johnny.

'Back him up. I'm on his side, so there.'

Harry laughed. 'Thanks, fat man. That makes me feel much better.'

'Thought it would,' said Billy Bunter, complacently. 'Nothing like having the most popular man in the Remove on your side. Don't go giving in.'

'I won't.'

'Good.' Bunter rolled inside. 'Don't let that beast Smithy throw his weight about. I'll tell you what, Wharton. If you want a better striker than Mauly, I'll play.'

'Ha, ha, ha!'

'Blessed if I see what you're cackling about,' said Bunter, indignantly. 'I wouldn't leave Harry in the lurch. Not my way. You stick to your guns, Harry. You'll be all right with me behind you.' His eyes gleamed as he approached the table. 'Oh, cake.'

'He must have known,' said Frank to Hurree.

'No, I didn't!' yelled Bunter. 'I never saw Gosling hand a parcel to Harry, and I never found the cake in the cupboard. That was why I didn't touch it. It was nothing to do with that beast Toddy finding me here. I wasn't looking for a cake, I was looking for a—a——'

'A cake?' suggested Hurree.

Bunter beamed at him. 'Thanks, old man,' he said. 'I wouldn't mind a piece.' He seized the knife and cut a wedge which left the cake in ruins, and munched away.

'Do think it over,' said Bob to Harry.

'No,' said Harry firmly. 'Smithy's not running the team, not unless the form elects him.'

'That's all very well,' argued Bob, 'but your job is to win matches, not lose them, and if anyone's going to score, it'll be Smithy.'

'No, it isn't, because he isn't going to play.'

'You let him alone, Bob Cherry.' Bunter's mouth was slightly muffled by cake. 'Smithy's a beast!'

'Shut up! No one asked for your opinion!' shouted Bob.

'Oh, really Cherry——'

'There's going to be trouble,' Frank said.

'You've already said so.'

'But don't you care?' asked Johnny.

'I couldn't care less.'

'Go on. Stick to it,' urged Bunter. 'Smack Smithy down. He ain't got no right to chuck dictionaries at people's chins.'

'Idiot!' said Frank.

Bunter glared at him. 'You're going a bit far,

Nugent.'

'Cretin!'

'Beast—no, no, didn't say that. I—I meant, that is, can I have another piece of cake?'

'You've only left a handful of crumbs. Shove them in your mouth, and then clear off,' said Harry.

Billy Bunter gave him an indignant blink, but he packed the remnants of the cake in his mouth. 'Don't worry,' he mumbled. 'I'll stand by you.'

There was the sound of feet coming up the passage, the door was flung open, and five of the team trampled in, their faces grim.

Squiff was in the lead. 'We've come to talk about the soccer team, Wharton,' he began.

'And what we think—' said Ogilvy.

'What we want to say—' said Morgan, at the same time.

'Why not speak one at a time,' said Harry, lightly. 'I might be able to follow you.'

'Look here,' they said together, and then stopped.

'Okay. Make it a chorus if you prefer it that way.'

Squiff gave Harry a hard look. 'You can probably guess what we've come to say.'

'Probably,' said Harry, easily.

'We want Smithy in the team. What are you going to do about it?'

'Nothing.'

'Even though everyone thinks you should?'

'That's right,' agreed Harry.

'Good old Harry!' squawked Bunter. 'Stand firm! I'm behind you. Don't let those oiks—yaroooo! Leggo my ear, Toddy, you beast! Ouch! Whatcher doing?' Toddy dragged the fat Owl to the door, and shoved him outside.

'We shan't have a hope of winning,' said Ogilvy, angrily. 'You're chucking the game away because Smithy got your back up. Well, it's not good enough.'

'If Smithy isn't playing, then we're not,' Toddy said.

'And you can take it or leave it,' added Russell.

Harry stared thoughtfully at them. 'You're giving me an ultimatum, are you?' he asked.

'You can put it like that,' replied Squiff.

'Fine. Would you mind shutting the door as you go out?'

Squiff and the others looked at each other. This wasn't what they had expected.

'Is that all you've got to say?' demanded Toddy.

'That's right. You've resigned. Did you want to say anything else?'

Silently, the wind completely taken out of their sails, the quintet left the study, and Toddy gave vent to his feelings by slamming the door hard behind him.

Harry's friends didn't speak as they watched him pull out a copy of the team list and draw lines through five of the names on it.

Frank spoke at last. 'You can't do it. You just can't.'

Harry looked up. 'What do you mean?' he asked.

'You can't take them all out of the team.'

'But I must. If they don't want to play, I can't make them.'

'But my dear Harry,' began Hurree Singh, 'they do want to play. If——'

'It didn't sound like that to me,' said Harry. He gazed round at his friends. 'It's a pity that we don't agree, isn't it? Anyway, I've got to think this out. I'd rather do it on my own, if you don't mind.'

They trooped out in silence, and Harry settled down to consider the problem.

Chapter 7

Bunter Courted

There was a smile on Vernon-Smith's face when he strolled into the common room before lunch on Wednesday. He and Redwing had come especially to see how Harry Wharton had plugged the gaps in the team.

Billy Bunter, sprawled in an armchair in a corner of the Rag, gave an angry blink through his big, round specs. His chin no longer ached, but he hadn't forgiven the Bounder for hurling that dictionary at him.

The blink was wasted. Smithy didn't even know that the Owl was there. He walked straight across to the notice board. 'What a crew!' he said derisively, looking at the list.

'It's hopeless,' said Redwing gloomily, 'and it's your fault, Smithy.'

'Mine? You're not going to give me another lecture, are you, Reddy? You're beginning to sound like a gramophone record!'

'But—' began Redwing.

'I can't help it if he won't meet me half way.' Smithy stared at the list again. 'What a joke! Look who he's put in. All he's got is a good goalie and a couple of strikers. The rest are a shower.'

'Oh, I don't know. Nugent's not all that bad——'

'And he's not all that good.'

'Dutton might do all right in midfield——'

'If he hears the ball coming,' jeered the Bounder.

'That's a filthy thing to say!'

'You know what I mean,' said Smithy, quickly. 'I know he can't help being a bit deaf, but he'll find it hard going.'

Redwing stared hard at the Bounder. 'I hope they do well,' he said.

'You can hope, but they'll only win if Courtfield die of laughing.'

'I don't think that's funny,' said Redwing. 'We're going to be licked, but——'

'You're telling me,' said the Bounder, grinning. 'They haven't got an earthly. Wharton might as well play Bunter. It wouldn't make much difference.'

Billy Bunter, deep in his armchair, gave Smithy a contemptuous blink, but like his earlier one, it was wasted.

Redwing became even more depressed. Smithy's fierce resentment about being left out the team had disappeared. Now he was enjoying the situation that he had created.

'If you think it's funny, you're about the only person who does. Wharton might be stubborn, but you've put him in a hopeless position and——'

'And that's where I'm going to keep him,' the Bounder said, triumphantly. 'He's a fool. He's playing straight into my hands. What do you think the form will say after the match? He'll have to resign or he'll be kicked out.'

Redwing caught his breath. 'And what have you got in mind, Smithy?' he asked quietly.

'If he asked me to play, I would.'

'Would you?'

'Yes, but he's not going to, is he?'

'I don't suppose so.'

'There you are. He's digging his own grave. There could be an election before long, and I'll tell you what, Redwing. I'm going to stand. I'm going to be a candidate. I wouldn't be surprised if I won.'

As he spoke, the Bounder's eyes sparkled. He hadn't set out to get rid of Wharton, but now that there was a good chance that he'd have to resign, he made up his mind to replace him. He hated playing second fiddle to anyone, and the idea of being the leader of the orchestra really appealed to him.

'What do you think? Like to see me as captain?' Redwing remained silent, and Smithy gave him a sharp look. 'You don't seem too keen on the idea, Reddy, but you'll back me just the same, won't you? I shall need every vote I can get.'

'I hope there won't be an election,' muttered Redwing.

'There will be,' said Smithy, confidently. 'I'll see to that. This has turned into a straight fight between Wharton and me.'

'But listen——'

'You listen to me. I thought Wharton was just letting off steam when he said he'd keep me out of the team, but he meant it. Do you think that I'm going to look on, standing around with my hands in my pockets like that yawning ass Mauly, or frowst in an armchair like that fat fool Bunter while the team's playing? No, Wharton's behaving like an ass, and I'm going to make the most of it.'

'There's no need to stir up more trouble.'

'Oh, no? You'll see. He's got a hopeless mob, but I'm not taking any chances. I'm going to make sure. I'm going to have a word with one or two more fellows.'

'Smithy! You can't!' Redwing looked appalled.

'Can't I? You'll see,' said the Bounder.

A fat voice came from the armchair. 'Yah! You won't get my vote, you rotten beast. I'll vote against you, see if I don't.'

The Bounder swung round. There was an angry glint in his eye, but suddenly it disappeared, and he smiled amiably at the fat Owl. 'Ah! You're just the chap I wanted to see, Bunter.'

'Well, I jolly well don't want to see your ugly mug,' said Bunter, warmly. 'I was only going to give you a message from Quelch, and you went and chucked that——'

'But I didn't know that,' said the Bounder. 'I was a

bit fed up at the time, but I shouldn't have done it, Bunter, old chap.'

Redwing listened in amazement. Smithy almost sounded as if he was apologising. What on earth was he up to?

'Anyway, Bunter, I was wondering——'

'You're a rotten beast!'

'I was wondering if you'd like to have tea in our study. We're going to have a bit of a spread. Come and share, Bunter.'

'Eh? What's that?' The Owl's grievances disappeared, and he positively beamed at the Bounder.

'Oh, well, Smithy, old man. Since you put it like that. I—I'm not the sort to bear grudges. You know me better than that. I'll come. I won't let you down.'

'That's fine.' Smithy gave the Owl a friendly nod, as he went out with Redwing.

'What's come over you, Smithy?'

The Bounder grinned. 'It's easy, isn't it, Reddy? I can count on his vote if there is an election.'

'But I don't think that——'

'You don't have to think,' said the Bounder, and he made his way into the quad, leaving Redwing frowning after him.

Chapter 8

Bunter in Demand Again

'Wharton!' Bolsover and Hazeldene spoke at the same time.

'Yes?'

Harry was in the quad with the rest of the Famous Five. Normally, the prospect of playing in a soccer match in the bright autumn sunshine would have made them cheerful, but they were all looking down in the mouth.

Bob Cherry felt peeved. He wasn't going to enjoy standing around with a painful knee, watching their third-rate team being beaten. Frank, although determined to do his best, knew that he wasn't good enough for the team, and Johnny was well aware that he'd have his work cut out to keep down the score. The Courtfield side would go through their defence like a knife through butter. Hurree Singh just hoped that they could at least mount an attack or two.

So, four of the Famous Five were hoping for the best, but expected the worst. It was hard to know what Harry Wharton was thinking. If he had doubts, he concealed them well. However, as Bolsover and Hazeldene approached, a shadow crossed his face. He scented trouble, and if there was any it would be because the Bounder had been busy again.

'Well, what is it?' Harry repeated.

'You see—' began Hazeldene, haltingly.

'Oh, I'll say it,' said Bolsover. 'Look, Wharton. We think that since you've turned Smithy out of the team——'

'Correction. Smithy turned himself out of the team.'

'And five others—' muttered Hazeldene.

'Haven't you heard?' said Harry, mildly. 'They resigned. They came specially up to my study to say so.'

'Oh, come off it!' snapped Bolsover. 'The truth is, you forced them into it. And now you're landed with a scratch side. We'll be the laughing stock of the school. If you refuse to play Smithy and Squiff and——'

'They're not playing,' said Harry, steadily.

'Then I'm not playing either, and neither is Hazeldene.'

'Is that right, Hazeldene?'

'Yes,' muttered Hazeldene. 'It's not good enough, Wharton. If you can do without them, then you can do without us.'

'Right,' said Harry, calmly. He took out the list

from his pocket once more, and crossed their names out. 'That's it. You can clear off.'

Bolsover and Hazeldene were astounded. They hadn't expected Harry to react like that, but since he'd turned his back on them, there was nothing they could do but leave.

'Oh, my best bonnet!' groaned Bob Cherry. 'It's getting madder and madder. Where are you going to get another defender and a midfield player from?'

'There's still a bit of talent knocking around,' Harry sounded unconcerned.

'But, Harry, you know that they'd all play if you put Smithy back in the team. Why don't you? There's still time.'

'Why not?' urged Frank.

'I'm not going all through that again, Frank.'

'You're making a mistake,' warned Johnny.

Harry gave him a cold look. 'Thinking of dropping out, are you?'

'Don't be such an ass!'

'Well, don't go on about it, old thing.' As he spoke, Harry glanced up at the clock tower. 'Kick off's at three,' he said. 'I haven't much time to rake up another couple of players. I'll have to get a move on. See you later.'

He gave his friends a quick smile and walked away, leaving them exchanging clouded glances. They were going to back him up—nothing would change that, but they felt that he shouldn't take such a hard line. Some of the fellows might have played if he had talked things over with them.

As it happened, as Harry made his way across the quad, he passed Squiff, Toddy and Ogilvy who were standing in a little group. They all looked up, perhaps hoping that things could still be put right, but he went by as if they didn't exist.

A few minutes later, he came across Skinner, Snoop and Stott lounging idly by the elms.

'Seen Elliott?' he asked.

Skinner grinned, delighted to be able to give bad news. 'He's gone out on his bike.'

Harry compressed his lips. 'Is Smith about?'

'He went out with Elliott.' Skinner winked, and Sidney James Snoop tittered.

Harry reflected that he was going to find it hard to find a couple of players at such short notice. He stood there, regarding Skinner and his two companions. Skinner and Snoop were lazy, but Stott quite enjoyed a game. If he hadn't been influenced by them, he might have been quite good. As it was, he was easily persuaded that games were a waste of time.

Harry made up his mind. 'Would you like to play this afternoon, Stott?' he said.

Stott looked startled. 'Funny you've never asked me before,' he said, a touch of sarcasm in his voice.

'But I am asking you now.'

'Because you're short of a player, I suppose,' put in Skinner.

'That's right. I need a defender. What about it, Stott?'

'Jolly flattering,' sneered Skinner. 'He'd never have asked you if he hadn't got to the bottom of the barrel.'

·'Anyway, he can't,' said Snoop. 'We were just going out. Coming, Stott?'

Stott gave Skinner and Snoop a slightly nervous glance, but he didn't move. 'Wharton's asked me to play.'

'So what? He's only come to you as a last resort.'

'I don't care,' said Stott. 'I'm going to play if I'm wanted.'

'You are,' said Harry.

Skinner sneered and Snoop frowned but, just for once, Stott seemed to have found some backbone. 'Okay,' he said. 'Count on me.'

'Good. Thanks,' replied Harry. 'I'll see you in the changing room. Don't be late.'

'I'll be there.'

As he walked off, he heard Skinner and Snoop arguing with Stott, but Stott put an end to it by striding off to get his football gear. This, however, was Harry's only success. Some of the Remove had gone out. Others, resentful that they were only being asked at the last minute, refused. One or two, realising that the team was bound to be beaten, turned him down.

Smithy, watching Harry going from one chap to another, wondered whether he'd be asked to play after all. Actually, it wouldn't have suited his books. Now he had the prospect of becoming the Remove captain, he was hoping that the team would be badly beaten.

Harry looked at his watch. The time was getting on and the Courtfield team were due to arrive at any moment, and still he hadn't got an eleventh player. He was becoming dispirited when he suddenly noticed a rotund figure lounging by the door of the changing room, blinking through his big, round spectacles.

For a split second, Harry hesitated. The team was already a hopeless ragbag, but there didn't seem to be any alternative. Bunter was his only hope.

'Bunter!' he said.

'I—I say, it wasn't me!' exclaimed Bunter, in alarm. 'I—I—I haven't been anywhere near your study, old man.'

'Listen!'

'Bub—bub—but it wasn't me. Couldn't have been. No idea you'd got a choc of box—no, no, a box of chocs in your study. Never opened the cupboard. Not me—wouldn't do anything like that, so——'

'Shut up, Bunter! Listen to me——'

'I—I bet you anything you like that it—it was Nugent who had those chocs—him or Smithy. Not that they were much to write home about—all soft centres, no nuts, nothing like that. That's why I didn't——'

'Like to play for the Remove?'

'Eh?' Billy Bunter jumped so violently, that his glasses almost slipped off his little button of a nose. 'What?'

'You offered to play the other day,' Harry reminded him. 'Well, now's your chance.'

'Oh, crikey!' breathed Bunter.

'Hazeldene's out. You'll have to play in midfield.'

'Oh,' said Bunter again. A grin spread across his fat face. He knew he was brilliant, even if no one else did. 'It's taken you a long time to get round to asking me, Wharton.'

'Are you playing?' demanded Harry.

'Since you're begging me to,' said Bunter, grandly, 'I will. You've got a lousy team, Wharton. But still, my talent will probably pull you through. You'll see.'

'Will I?'

'Yes,' said the Owl, confidently. 'We'll beat the Courtfield mob with me in the team.'

Worried though he was, Harry couldn't help laughing. 'Right. Roll into the changing room and get changed, barrel.'

Bunter gave a sniff. 'I suppose you'll still want to lead the team out,' he said. 'It ought to be the best player by rights, but I expect that you're much too petty to let me have my little spot of glory.

'That's right,' said Harry, briskly. 'Now get a move on. It's almost time for kick off.'

Chapter 9

Seven–One!

Bob Cherry groaned. It wasn't because his damaged knee was hurting. It was because the match between Courtfield juniors and the Remove was turning out to be a disaster.

He wasn't alone on the sideline. Quite a lot of the

Remove had gathered to watch, including the discarded members of the team. Vernon-Smith was the only one without a grim face, although he tried to conceal his delight as the Courtfield team swept through the defences yet again.

There were people from other forms too. The news that there had been trouble in the Remove had spread, and the fact that Billy Bunter was in the team had caused quite a lot of hilarity. Temple and his friends in the fourth had turned up, and they agreed that it was more like a circus than a soccer match.

The Remove were particularly unfortunate. While their team was at its weakest, the Courtfield side was at its best. Trumper, their captain, had warned them to expect a hard match, but his strikers smashed their way through the Remove's feeble defence time and time again.

'What a laugh!' whispered the Bounder to Redwing.

'Shut up!'

'It's a pantomime!'

Redwing frowned at the Bounder. He knew that he was partly to blame, but that Smithy was even more guilty. He watched with a dismal face, conscious of the Bounder's sardonic amusement, and he felt irritated by him.

The game was entertaining from one point of view. The Remove had never played a worse game, and never had so many chaps on the same side collided with each other so frequently.

There were one or two bright spots, but they hardly compensated for the team's poor performance. Johnny Bull performed miracles, considering that their defence was hopeless. Shots rained down, and as Skinner remarked, it looked as if the Courtfield juniors might easily score a century, but somehow he blocked most of them.

The midfield players did their best, but they were

. . . THE BALL HIT ITS TARGET.

struggling, and one of them spent most of his time sitting on the ground, groaning loudly. In fact, every time that the fat Owl fell over, he took longer and longer to get onto his fat, little legs again.

Harry Wharton, a grim look on his face, worked tirelessly, as if determined to snatch victory out of defeat, while Hurree and Frank did all they could to back him up.

But the real eye-opener, was the performance of Lord Mauleverer. Everyone had thought that he might be marginally better than Bunter, but they were all quite wrong. He was keen and alert, playing up as if soccer was the most important thing in his life.

Ten minutes before the end of the first half, Courtfield were three goals up, and as the whistle went to restart the game, they tore down onto the home goal like wolves on a fold. There was a scramble in the goal mouth. Johnny managed to grab the ball, bounced it, and kicked it to one of his midfield players.

There was a yell as the ball hit its target. 'Ow! Wow! Yarooo!' Billy Bunter landed with a thud on the ground, and clutched his chest and he rolled over and over.

Tom Dutton tackled a Courtfield player, got possession of the ball, and sent it with a sideways flick to Harry, who quickly passed to Hurree, and then raced up the pitch. The ball went from Hurree to Mauly, and Mauly, with an ease and grace that no one suspected him capable of, dribbled past two men, and sent a short, accurate pass to Harry, who slammed the ball into the corner of the net.

'Goal!' yelled the Bounder, temporarily forgetting his ambitions.

'Goal!' roared Redwing, with relief.

'Goal!' bellowed Bob Cherry, hopping up and down in his excitement, completely forgetting his bruised knee.

But then Smithy remembered that victory would

ruin his plans. 'It was just a flash in the pan,' he said scornfully.

He wasn't far out. By half time, the score was four to one, and during the interval, a fat, winded figure crawled off the pitch and wasn't seen again for the rest of the game. Keen though Billy Bunter had been to play, he was now far keener to get off that beastly pitch. Dripping with perspiration and aching in every limb, hopelessly winded, and almost dead with fatigue, he stealthily made his way back to the Rag, an armchair, and a box of Ogilvy's toffees.

Long before the end of the game, Harry Wharton knew that, in spite of all their efforts, the game was lost. Luckily, Johnny was still a tower of strength. But for his stubborn and tireless defence, the score would have been in double figures. It was seven–one when the final whistle went. There had never been a bigger defeat in the history of Greyfriars.

After the opposing team had left, Harry made his way to the Rag, well aware that there was going to be a lot of criticism, but determined to face the music. There was a faint hiss, and an odd boo as he entered.

The Remove felt humiliated by their team's dismal performance, particularly since so many other members of the school had been watching. Up till now, they had prided themselves on being sportsmen who could take defeat in their stride, but they hadn't just been defeated; they had been annihilated.

Harry flushed, but his expression didn't change. The Bounder, standing in a corner, nudged Redwing. He was there, ready to stir up trouble if necessary, but there was no need for it. The form was in a ferment, convinced that they had lost because of Wharton's pride and high-handed behaviour.

'He's for it!' Smithy whispered, excitedly.

'It's rough on Wharton,' muttered Redwing.

'Yes?' jeered the Bounder. 'He won't give an inch. He'd rather see the team lose match after match than let me play. No one's going to stand for that. He deserves what's coming.'

Mauly, stretched out in an armchair, quite overcome by his unusual and strenuous exertions, sat up straight, and smiled and nodded at Harry. It was the only friendly greeting.

A number of others, gave Harry black looks, and looked as if they'd like to lay hands on him.

'Look here, Harry—' whispered Frank.

'Well?'

'There's no point in having a row now. Why not wait until things have cooled down. Let's get out of this.'

Wharton smiled, and shook his head.

'You've put their backs up,' grunted Johnny Bull. 'Leave it for now.'

'It's no good talking to them now,' muttered Bob.

'No time like the present.'

'My dear Harry, leave it until later,' urged Hurree.

Wharton took no notice. He had something to say, and he was determined to do it. He stood, his hands in his pocket, with an air of cool indifference that infuriated the Remove. As Squiff, Toddy, Ogilvy and one or two others came towards him, there was another boo.

'Oh, shut up!' exclaimed Squiff, looking round. 'Let me speak. Look here, Wharton——'

'Yes?'

'We need never have lost that match.'

'I bet Courtfield laughed all the way home,' said Toddy.

'You must be proud of yourself,' sneered Ogilvy. 'Seven to one. That's quite a record.'

There was a babble of voices, and Harry waited until it died down. 'You seem to be a bit upset,' he remarked, quite casually.

'A bit upset!' repeated Squiff. 'You turned the best striker out of the side——'

'Your memory's failing, Squiff. If you mean Vernon-Smith, he turned himself out.'

'He was ready to play,' said Toddy, angrily. 'You wouldn't let him, just because he'd got your back up.'

'No! That's not true. I warned him of what would happen, and he ignored the warning. As long as I'm captain, what I said still stands.'

The Bounder smiled triumphantly, and gave Redwing a wink. Things were going just the way he wanted them to.

'That's what we were talking about when you came in.'

'I didn't need a crystal ball to guess that,' replied Harry. 'There's someone here who'll be only too glad to replace me,' and he gave the Bounder a cool glance. 'You might pull it off, Vernon-Smith, unless you're sacked first.' As the Bounder went red, Harry continued, 'Don't worry. I'm not staying where I'm not wanted.' He faced the crowd. 'You all know what I intend to do. Either I run the team my way, or not at all. You can take it or leave it.'

'Harry—' muttered Frank.

'That's what I came here to say. I'll resign here and now, if that's what you want. You can choose.'

'I guess we've chosen already,' said Squiff. He looked round the room. 'Am I right? We want you to go.'

There was a roar of approval. A gentle 'No' came from Mauly, but it was drowned in general uproar. There was no doubt about the feeling in the Remove.

'Well?' snapped Squiff. 'What have you got to say to that?'

'Nothing,' said Harry, with the same cool air of indifference. 'It's all right by me. I resign,' and he turned on his heels and walked out of the Rag.

Chapter 10
Back Up!

'I hope Bob gets a move on,' said Johnny. 'I'm starving.'

It was the day following the match, and it was tea time. There was quite a spread in study no 1. There was ham and there was jam, there were doughnuts and eggs, and Johnny had contributed a very large cake.

The door opened. 'I say, you fellows!' Bunter blinked in.

Frank groaned. 'He's got a nose like a bloodhound.'

Surprisingly, the Owl didn't even glance at the table. Normally, his round, little eyes would have gleamed with anticipation, and his eager paws would have stretched out for the goodies, but for about the first time in his life, he ignored them. Food, it seemed, was of no interest.

'I've just looked in——'

'Then look out again!' snapped Johnny.

'Oh, really, Bull——'

'And shut the door after you,' said Frank.

'Oh, really, Nugent——'

'What do you want?' asked Harry. 'If it's tea——'

'I rather think that our fat friend has already had tea.'

'Eh? How do you know that?' asked Billy Bunter.

'My dear Bunter,' replied Hurree Singh. 'Do not think that it is because you have smears of jam around your mouth, crumbs on your blazer, and cream on your trousers.'

'Oh?' Bunter looked perplexed.

'It is the fact that your hands are still in your pockets instead of reaching for our cake.'

There was a roar of laughter, and Bunter said, huffily, 'I don't see what you're cackling about.'

'What are you after?' asked Harry.

'Nothing from you, Wharton. Wouldn't get it, not after the row you've had with Smithy.' He produced a crumpled piece of paper and a stub of pencil. 'I've come to talk to the others.' He grinned round at them. 'What I want to know is, who's going to vote for Smithy? I've got some names already.'

'Vote for Smithy!' exclaimed Harry. So far, no matter what had happened, he had managed to remain outwardly cool, but the flush that appeared on his face showed that he wasn't as indifferent to Smithy's tactics as he had pretended to be.

'That's it,' said the Owl, importantly. 'I'm going round canvassing for votes—see who's on his side. He's my dandicate—no, no, candidate.'

'Get out, you stupid twit!' said Frank.

'Oh, I say, Nugent.' Bunter licked his pencil. 'The election's today. Went to a meeting in Smithy's study——'

'With jam and cake,' said Hurree.

'What? Well, there were some light refreshments,' said Bunter, grandly. 'But I didn't go there for that. Went to help.'

'And helped yourself.' said Johnny, sourly.

'Me? I hope I know better than to gorge myself at another chap's table, but you should have seen Skinner and Snoop digging in. Guzzled all the jam tarts, they did. Only got four or five myself. Do you know,' he went on confidentially, 'I saw Fishy slipping some apples into his pocket. Tee, hee, hee!'

'And you didn't?' asked Frank.

'Course not. I'm not greedy like some chaps I know.'

'Then what's that bulging in your blazer pocket?'

'Tain't an apple. Ain't a pear neither. Couldn't. Fishy took those, too.'

'Then it's a lump of cake,' suggested Frank.

Billy Bunter glared at him. 'How did you know

that? Anyway, it's only a small bit.' He chuckled again. 'Smithy's not so bad, is he? I mean, he's got his good points——'

'Like he's a good shot with a dictionary,' said Johnny.

'I'm not like some. I don't bear grudges,' said Bunter, with a dignified air.

'I am sure that you don't, my dear Bunter, not when there's jam and cake about.'

'That's nothing to do with it.' The Owl sounded offended. 'Tain't because he lent me fifty pence neither——'

'Ha, ha, ha!'

'Stop sounding like a pack of hyenas,' snapped Bunter. 'I tell you, Smithy's going to make a jolly good captain. He ain't going to be high and mighty like you, Wharton.'

'Really?'

'Smithy's more understanding. He's not going to make people turn out for compulsory games like you. He'll be a bit more sympathetic when I've got a touch of plumbago. You always rooted me out, you know you did.'

'That's right,' agreed Harry.

'Don't think I've got anything against you, old man, but you always were a bit of a beast. It'll be much better. Lots of chaps think so. I say, have you heard that Toddy's standing? Ought to have backed him up since we share a study,' and Bunter shook his head sadly. 'Pity, but he couldn't expect it, not when he's so jolly mean about grub. Do you know what he did when I told him? He kicked me——'

'Good!' said Johnny.

'Beast! Oh, no. I—I mean, you're going to rally round Smithy, aren't you? Tell you what, I'll put your names down, shall I? It'll be worth your while.'

'You paunchy parrot!' roared Johnny.

Bunter's eyes flickered nervously behind his specs.

'But—but you don't understand, Bull. Smithy's going, to put on a super spread to celebrate his election. Not that it's anything to do with voting. He made that quite clear. Still, he's asking everyone who's on his side. You don't want to miss that, do you? After all, Smithy's loaded with cash.'

Harry Wharton gave a short laugh. Smithy wasn't being over scrupulous about his electioneering methods, and he had already turned the fat Owl into an enthusiastic supporter.

'Oh, you can titter, Wharton,' said Bunter, petulantly, 'but you'll be sorry. Smithy's spreads aren't to be sneezed at. Look here, I can't hang about. The election's at seven. Wingate's coming in to count the votes. I've got Skinner, Snoop and Stott on my list, as well as Bolsover and Fishy. Do you want your name down, Bull?'

'If you do, I'll boot you!'

'Beast! What about you, Frank, old man?'

'Don't bother!'

'Huh! Come on, Hurree. Let me put you down,' urged Bunter.

'I think not.'

'You'll be sorry.'

'On the contrary, I think you will.'

'What? You don't know Smithy,' Bunter said, warmly. He turned to Harry. 'Ain't no good asking you, I suppose?'

'You suppose right.'

'I wish you'd think about it,' said Bunter, peevishly. 'He'll make a jolly good captain, and he's smashing at soccer. He won't play a load of duds like you did, Wharton. If you ask me, there was only good man in the team. Don't want to boast——'

'Ha, ha, ha!'

'Oh, don't keep on cackling whenever I open my mouth,' yapped Bunter. 'Look, you can't vote for a mean beast like Toddy. Smithy's streets ahead of him.

I'm plumping for him, and so are lots of others. It'll be worth your while. Back me up.'

Johnny Bull got up. 'You want me to back you up, do you?'

'Rather!' said the Owl, enthusiastically.

'Right!'

'Good!' beamed Bunter. 'Good for you. Glad you've got a bit of sense in your thick head. You back— why—what? Leggo! Wharrer you up to, you great oaf? Ugh!' He let out a terrified squawk as Johnny grasped his shoulders and shoved him against the wall of the study. 'Ow! Wow! Must be off your rocker! Ow! Leggo!'

'I'll show you just how I'm going to back you up, you podgy parasite!' growled Johnny.

'Yoohooop! Stoppit! Warrgh! Yaarooo!' yelled Bunter, as his head was cracked against the wall. 'Beast! Yaaah!' The fat Owl squirmed away from Johnny, and bolted for the door. He'd had all the backing he wanted from study no 1.

He rubbed his sore head, and trundled slowly up the Remove passage, a disgruntled expression on his face, but it disappeared as he saw Bob Cherry coming towards him.

He came to a halt, his ample figure almost blocking the passage. 'Hold on, old man,' he said.

Bob shook his head. 'Sorry, old pancake, but there's nothing doing.'

Billy Bunter was puzzled. 'What's what? What do you mean?'

'I'm skint. Stoney broke.'

'Tain't that,' said Bunter. 'Nothing like that, Cherry. I know where I can get a little loan if my postal order doesn't turn up. No, I'm on about something different. I'm canvassing, Bob, old man. Getting votes for Smithy. He's a decent chap, Smithy is.'

'Changed has he, since he clonked you on the chin with that dictionary?'

'Oh, that don't matter,' said Bunter, airily. 'The only thing I want is to see the best man win, and that's Smithy. He'll do better than Wharton, I can tell you that.'

'That's a laugh!'

Billy Bunter blinked up and down the passage. 'There ain't no one about, so you can come clean, Cherry. I bet you got fed up with Wharton, same as everyone else.'

Bob glowered at him. 'Get out of the way, you cackling clown!'

'Beast! That—that is, shall I put your name down?'

'You're out of your tiny mind, Bunter.'

'But if you let me,' said the Owl, eagerly. 'I'll see that you get an invite to his spread after he's won.'

'You fat frabjous, footling, flabby flounder! It's lucky for you that my knee's not better, or I'd boot you down the passage.'

Billy Bunter gave him an angry blink, and then, as Bob gave his knee a little rub, he grinned. 'That still giving you trouble?'

'What do you think?'

'Is it really bad?'

'Would I be limping around if it wasn't?'

Bunter looked hurt. 'There's no need to yell, Cherry. I was only asking. Could you run up the passage if you wanted to?'

'I couldn't run a yard.'

'That's tough,' said the Owl, sympathetically. 'So if a fellow smacked you on the kisser for calling him names, you couldn't do anything about it?'

'No—ow! Wow!' bellowed Bob, as a fat paw suddenly shot out and punched his nose. 'Why, you—you—you—I—I——'

'Tee, hee, hee!' tittered Bunter, leaping away, and scuttling up the passage.

'You bloated balloon!' Bob took one long stride, but the pain in his leg brought him to a standstill. 'Ouch!'

he gasped. 'Ouch!'

There was a distant cackle. 'Hee, hee, hee!'

Billy Bunter, still chuckling, disappeared, and Bob Cherry, with feelings that were too deep for words, limped towards study no 1, and tea.

Chapter 11

The Election

'The place is packed,' remarked Bob, as the Famous Five went into the Rag just before seven that evening.

'Wharton!'

'Yes?' Harry glanced round.

A small group of fellows were clustered round Toddy, who was beckoning Wharton over to his side of the room. Although Harry didn't move, a lazy figure emerged from an armchair and sauntered over to join them. Mauly brought Toddy's supporters up to seven.

There was quite a little crowd surrounding the Bounder on the other side of the room. There were chaps like Squiff, Russell and Ogilvy, as well as slackers like Skinner and his friends.

'I think we ought to support Toddy,' said Bob. 'He's our man.' Wharton raised his eyebrows. 'Is he?' he asked.

'Well, he might not turn out to be brilliant as captain, but we want to keep Smithy out, don't we?'

'Do we?' murmured Harry.

'Well, don't we?' demanded Johnny Bull, warmly. 'Didn't Smithy start the trouble? Now he's cashing in on it.'

'Yes.' Harry sounded remote.

'Well then—' said Frank.

Wharton shrugged. 'If they want Smithy, they can have him.'

'My dear Harry, surely it would be better to vote for Toddy,' said Hurree Singh.

'Do what you like. I'll watch.'

'But Harry!' protested Frank. 'Do you mean that you're not going to vote?'

'Yes.'

'But—' began Johnny and Bob at the same time.

Harry cut them short. 'I've made up my mind.' He strolled over to Mauly's armchair, sat down, crossed his legs and folded his arms, looking with mild interest at the scene.

Johnny grunted. 'Come on,' he said to the others, and they walked in a bunch to Toddy's supporters.

Toddy grinned welcomingly at them. 'On my side?'

'It looks like it,' said Bob. 'At least you're better than that snake Smithy.'

'What about Wharton?'

'He's opted out,' grunted Johnny.

Bob glanced round. 'How many can you count on?'

'Eleven, including you lot. One or two more might drift this way, but I'm not sure. At least Smithy isn't going to have a walkover.'

Bob looked round the noisy Rag, and he began to count heads. 'Nearly everyone's here. Let's see, twenty-three, twenty-four. What do you make it, Frank?'

'Twenty-six, I think.'

'I'm a bit unlucky,' remarked Toddy. 'Linley, Penfold and Brown aren't here. I'd have got at least two of their votes.'

'Well, if Harry's not going to take part, there are twenty-three since you and Smithy are out of it. You've got nearly half, Toddy.'

'Mm! It's going to be close. Still, it looks as if Smithy's going to get the odd vote unless Harry plumps for me. Can't you persuade him?'

'Not a hope,' said Johnny.

Toddy glanced at his watch. 'It's nearly time,' he

said.

'Wingate will be here in a tick,' said Bob. 'I say, Squiff,' he shouted across the room. 'You're in the wrong queue. That bus is only going back to the garage. Come and join us.'

'Not likely. Yours doesn't look as if it's going to start.'

'Hallo, hallo, hallo!' Bob bawled to Billy Bunter. 'Roll over here, barrel. I'll tell you what. I'll do you a good turn. I'll cash your next postal order.'

'Yah!'

As the clock struck seven, the door of the Rag opened, and Wingate entered. He looked round at the crowd of excited juniors before closing the door again.

Harry Wharton, still seated in the armchair, looked on with an air of complete indifference. Toddy gave him an appealing look, and Smithy scowled, but neither produced a flicker of emotion.

'Look at him!' Vernon-Smith muttered in Redwing's ear. 'He's getting a kick out of this.'

Redwing looked surprised. 'What do you mean? You've got one more than Toddy. What are you worrying about? It looks as if Wharton doesn't intend to take part.'

'Oh, don't be so thick!' snapped the Bounder. 'I know what he's getting up to. He'll join Toddy at the last moment so it'll be a tie. He wants to see me squirm.'

'So what?' It'll just mean that we'll have another election later on. Some of Toddy's crew might change their minds and come over to you.'

'And I might lose some of mine,' hissed Smithy. 'That prig Linley will be back, and so will Penfold and Brown. They'll probably vote for Toddy. If I don't pull it off now, I might never do it. Wharton's a rat. He's deliberately sitting there, keeping me on tenderhooks——'

'Of course he isn't. He isn't like that.'

'Don't be such a fool!' The Bounder clenched his fists as he looked at that cool, still figure in the armchair. He gave him another black look, and was even more annoyed when he received a polite smile in return.

Wingate climbed onto a chair, and held up his hand. Slowly, the din died away. 'Are you all ready?' he asked. 'Right, let's get down to it?' I want to know who's proposing and who is seconding each candidate. Fine,' he went on, as hands were raised. 'I'll give you just a couple more minutes in case any of you have second thoughts.' No one moved. 'Hands up for Vernon-Smith.'

Twelve hands shot into the air, one of them badly in need of washing, and then another dirty hand was raised.

'What do you think you're doing?' demanded Wingate. 'You know perfectly well that it's one man, one vote, Bunter!'

Trying to wangle two invitations to Smithy's spread,' said Bob.

'Right. Twelve votes for Vernon-Smith. Now, hands up for Peter Todd.'

Eleven hands were raised, and all eyes turned to Harry Wharton, but he sat there, mildly interested, but not really concerned.

The Bounder caught his breath. 'Is he really going to stay put?'

'It looks like it.'

The Bounder could hardly control his excitement. 'I think I'm going to make it.'

Wingate, aware that Harry had not voted, looked at him, but still he didn't stir. Slowly, he began counting.

'Get a move on,' hissed Smithy, between his teeth.

'Right, eleven,' said Wingate, and there an excited buzz. 'Vernon-Smith, twelve votes, Todd, eleven votes. I declare that Vernon-Smith is captain of the Remove!'

Chapter 12
Nothing for Bunter

Billy Bunter sneered. It was one of his best efforts, large and expressive. He curled a fat lip, and he turned up a fat little nose, and his little round eyes blinked scorn through his large, round specs.

He was standing in his study, regarding the tea table. Bunter seldom scorned food of any sort, and so his attitude was surprising. It was true that study no 7 was seldom overflowing with goodies like the Bounder's or Lord Mauleverer's. Peter Todd and Tom Dutton were far from wealthy, and although, according to Bunter, his palatial home at Bunter Court was a luxurious establishment, none of its luxuries ever trickled through to Greyfriars.

But still, although study No 7 didn't have much in the way of food, Bunter was always there to make sure that he had his fair share—and a bit more if he could get his fat paws on it. Now, on the day following the election, his behaviour was quite remarkable. He didn't sit down and he didn't stretch out a podgy hand, but he did stand in the doorway with a fat sneer on his face.

'That all you've got for tea, Toddy?' he asked, disdainfully.

'That's it, dustbin,' said Peter. 'What's wrong? Not enough?'

'Not enough?' sneered Bunter. 'It's pathetic.'

'You could nip down to the tuckshop and try to improve it. We'll wait until you get back.'

'Oh, really, Toddy!'

Tom Dutton looked at Bunter. 'You've got a nerve, showing your fat face in here. If I were Toddy, I'd boot you. You ought to be ashamed of yourself—voting against your study-mate.'

'Pooh!' sniffed Bunter. 'I voted for the best man, and I jolly well got him in. He ain't half grateful. He's a jolly good sort. Look at the spread he gave last night. He'll make a first-class skipper.'

'Eh?' Dutton looked at the table. 'Where's the kipper?'

'Not kipper!' shouted Bunter. 'Skipper!'

'A slipper? What are you on about?'

'Oh, for goodness sake——'

'Cake? There isn't one. Do you need new specs? We haven't got a kipper and we haven't got a cake, and I don't know why you're wittering on about slippers. If you want kippers and cake, you can jolly well go and get them. It would make a change.'

'That's right,' said Toddy.

'I would have done,' said Bunter. 'You know I would, but I didn't get that postal order I was counting on. I told you, Toddy, that one was on its way——'

'Yes. Lots of times.'

'But if that's all you've got for tea, I'm not staying here,' and the Owl blinked scornfully at the table yet again. 'Bread and butter, and a few miserable sardines—Yah! I know where I'm welcome.'

'Good! Roll off!' said Peter, cheerfully. 'There'll be more for us. Close the door.'

'Yah!' snorted Bunter again, as he banged the door of the study, and he bowled up the passage to study no 4.

There was a smile on his face and a gleam of happy anticipation in his eyes as he reached it. Now that he had become Smithy's close friend, he could afford to turn up his nose at the supplies in his own study. He had no doubt that Smithy would welcome him with open arms.

He tapped at the door, pushed it open, and blinked in. Smithy and Redwing were seated at the lavishly spread table, and his grin became broader.

Smithy was looking pleased with himself. He was the Remove captain, and Harry Wharton was nothing more than a back number. Success was meat and drink to the Bounder. It was true that he had won by only a very narrow margin, but that didn't matter. Victory was victory. He was speaking as the fat Owl peered round the door, and he went on talking enthusiastically to Redwing.

'I'm going to be able to select a really good team for the Rookwood match. Linley, Browney and Penfold will be back, and Bob Cherry's knee will have mended. We'll be a really strong side.'

'I say, Smithy!' squeaked Bunter.

The Bounder looked round. 'Shut that door!'

'Oh, really, Smithy——'

'What do you want then?'

Billy Bunter blinked reproachfully. Surely Smithy didn't need to ask. Practically everyone knew what it meant when the fat Owl rolled into a chap's study at tea time.

'I—I—What I thought, Smithy, was—was that I'd just give you a look in.'

'Well, now that you've looked in, you can look out again, you fool. Push off!'

'I—I say, I'm jolly glad you won yesterday, old man. I—I was so keen that you'd have got an extra vote off me if Wingate hadn't spotted what I was up to.'

'You stupid ass!'

Bunter gazed longingly at the tea table, and edged a little further into the room. 'Well, we pulled it off,' he squeaked. 'Wharton's nose is properly out of joint, ain't it? Hee, hee, hee! Don't want to boast, but my canvassing paid off. Made a chap hungry, all that footwork, calling at all those studies. I—I—I say. That reminds me. I—I haven't had tea yet'

'Really?' The Bounder got to his feet. 'Wait a minute while I get something out of the cupboard.'

'Oh!' Bunter's eyes gleamed. 'Would—would it be a cake, Smithy?'

'No, it's something I've been keeping specially for you.'

Bunter beamed. 'That's jolly decent of you, Smithy.'

'Shan't be a tick.' The Bounder groped in the cupboard.

'Don't!' said Redwing sharply, as he saw what Smithy had in his hands.

'Oh!' Bunter had been rolling in, but he suddenly stopped rolling as he spotted the bag of flour, and he gave the Bounder an anxious blink. 'But—but—look here, you beast, that is, Smithy, old man,' he babbled. 'Didn't I jolly well vote for you? If—if it hadn't been for me, you wouldn't have got in. I could have voted for Toddy. You only scraped in by one vote, you know you did, and you're jolly mean, too. All that grub—don't ask a chap who got you elected—I say, keep off, you beast!'

As the Bounder approached him, the fat Owl bounded backwards like a kangaroo, and banged the door. 'Beast!' he howled through the keyhole. 'Rotten, stingy beast!'

It was a disconsolate Bunter that trudged back to his own study, his vision of spreads in Smithy's study fading like a mirage in the desert. He was forced to face the fact that Smithy had no further use for him.

Peter Todd grinned as the fat Owl trundled in. 'I thought you were having tea with your chum Smithy.'

Billy Bunter gave an indignant snort. 'I've done with that rotter,' he said. 'He's a rotter and a cad. I jolly well wish I'd voted for you, Toddy. After all, we've always been pals. I've been thinking about it. I'd much rather have tea with you.'

'Would you?' said Toddy, amused.

'Yes, old chap,' said Bunter, with real feeling. He blinked towards the table, and his jaw dropped.

'Crumbs!'

He hadn't been away long, but there was very little left except for half a loaf.

'Oh, crikey!'

'Sit down, old fruit cake,' said Toddy hospitably. 'Help yourself.'

'But there ain't much left,' said Bunter, miserably. 'I—I say, Peter, is there anything in the cupboard?'

'Yes,' said Toddy. 'You can have it.'

'Oh, thanks.' Eagerly, the fat Owl opened the cupboard door, and uttered a howl of rage. 'You rotten beast, Toddy!' He turned round, a tin of shoe polish in his hands, and he flung it petulantly in Toddy's direction before rolling off again in the hope of finding someone who would fill that aching void in his stomach.

Chapter 13

The New Broom

'Little Side at three! Don't be late.'

Herbert Vernon-Smith flung the words at the Famous Five after lunch on Saturday, and walked on down the passage without waiting for a reply.

They turned and stared at each other. Bob Cherry frowned, Nugent breathed rather hard, Hurree shrugged his shoulders, and Johnny Bull grunted. Harry Wharton gave a faint smile.

'Cheeky blighter!' said Bob.

'I suspect,' said Hurree, 'that it will not be long before he has to buy a new hat. His head is swelling.'

'Does he think that we're slackers like Skinner and his mob?' declared Johnny.

'No. He just wants to throw his weight around,' said Frank. 'I've got a good mind not to turn up.'

'Can't do that,' Bob reminded him. 'It's compulsory games.'

'I know, but all the same——'

'Take it easy,' said Harry Wharton. 'We don't want to be reported to Wingate, do we?'

'He's got to round everyone up,' remarked Bob, 'but he could be a bit more civil about it instead of sounding like a sergeant major.'

Smithy was enjoying his sense of power, and he had particularly enjoyed snapping out an order to Harry Wharton, even if there was no need for it since the Famous Five would never dream of missing games.

Knowing that he had left them feeling annoyed, and rather amused by it, the Bounder looked in on study no 14. Fisher T. Fish had a sheet of paper covered in figures in front of him, and a pen in his hands. The businessman of the Remove was busy with his accounts. He glanced up irritably as the door was opened.

'Games practice at three,' said the Bounder, tersely.

'So what?' snapped Fishy. 'Can't you see I'm busy? I didn't vote for you for nothing, Smithy.'

'Too bad. If you're not there, Wingate will want to know why.' The Bounder turned away, leaving Fishy fuming.

He made his way to study no 12, where Mauly was stretched out on his sofa, gazing rather vacantly out of the window.

'Turn up at Little Side at three!' he snapped.

Mauly glanced up. 'Is it compulsory games?'

'You ought to know.'

'Find it a bit difficult to remember things like that.'

'Then you'd better remember, or I shall report you to Wingate.'

As the Bounder slammed the door shut, Mauly got up reluctantly, a pained expression on his face. 'Fellow's getting above himself,' he said.

Smithy marched on to study no 11. Snoop and Stott gave him welcoming grins as he appeared in the doorway. 'Glad you've popped in,' said Skinner, amiably. 'We're going out this afternoon. Coming?'

'Not a hope,' said Smithy, briskly. 'It's games practice at three.'

Skinner laughed. 'Bad luck,' he said. 'I suppose you can hardly cut it now you're captain. It's got its penalties, hasn't it? I guess that Wingate would notice if you weren't there.'

'Tough!' said Snoop.

'Yes. Hard cheese,' agreed Stott.

Undoubtedly, the three of them had been given the impression by Smithy that life was going to be a lot easier for them if they voted for him.

'I thought I'd better warn you.'

'Pity,' said Skinner, easily. 'I can see that it wouldn't do for you to be absent. What we thought we'd do was——'

'Then stop thinking,' said the Bounder. 'Get down to the changing rooms. I'll see you on Little Side at three sharp.'

'What?'

'What's got into you?'

'Who do you think you're talking to?'

'You heard!' The Bounder turned to leave.

Snoop and Stott stared at each other in amazement, and Skinner got to his feet, an unpleasant glitter in his eyes. 'Just hold on a minute, Smithy.'

'Well?' said the Bounder, impatiently.

'It's a joke, isn't it?'

'No.'

'Come off it, Smithy.' Skinner's voice was harsh. 'You know very well why we voted for you. You can let us off games, and we expect you to. We counted on it.'

'Tough on you,' said the Bounder.

'But you led us to believe——'

'More than that,' put in Snoop. 'You as good as said——'

The Bounder gave them a mocking smile. 'Really? You must have misunderstood me. Little Side at three! Anyone who isn't there will be reported to Wingate.'

'Look here, you rotter—' began Skinner, furiously.

'I can't waste time on slackers like you.'

'You'll be sorry——'

'Will I?' Smithy gave them a scornful glance, and left.

In study no 7, he found the fattest member of the Remove stretched out in an armchair, a jammy smile on his face, and a jam tart poised in the air.

Bunter blinked in alarm as the door opened, and hastily crammed the jam tart into his mouth. 'I—I say, it—it wasn't me,' he mumbled, 'I—I thought you were Russell. Not that I've been anywhere near his study, but—but he might just have thought that this was his jam tart because he did have some and now he hasn't. That is, jam tarts look alike, don't they? Who—who can tell if mine is his or——'

'On your feet!' ordered the Bounder.

'Whaffor?' demanded the Owl.

'You ought to know. It's games at three. There'll be trouble if you don't turn up.'

'But—but—' stammered the Owl. 'You—you can let me off. You know you can. After all, I jolly well voted for you. Used my influence—ain't going to harrass me like Wharton did, are you? You—you can excuse me. You've got the power——'

'That's right,' said Smithy, with an unpleasant laugh, 'and I'm using it.'

'Oh, but really, Smithy——'

'Get moving!'

'But—but tain't three. Anyway——'

'I know it isn't three, but I'm not coming up here again. Move yourself.'

'I—I can't,' groaned Bunter. 'Tain't that I wouldn't. I can't. I'm not fit.'

'Then a bit of exercise will make all the difference.'

'I—I don't mean that. I've—I've got this awful pain,

Smithy,' said the Owl pathetically.

'You'll have a worse one if you don't get your fat carcass off that chair.'

'But—but it really is bad,' protested Bunter. 'You—you don't know what it's like. I—I think it's appendicitis of the knee. That or plumbago. I was going to matron about it. I—I think I ought to see a doctor. You understand, don't you, Smithy? I'm not slacking. Not me. Wouldn't. It's just that my leg's playing up—after all, we're pals, always have been, haven't we?'

'No!'

'What?' hooted Bunter.

'We haven't been pals, and you've always been a slacker,' said the Bounder. 'Well, that's going to stop!' and he advanced on the Owl.

Billy Bunter tried to huddle deeper in the armchair as Smithy loomed over him. 'But—but—look here, you beast—yaroooo! Leggo my ear! If you don't leggo my ear, I'll—wow! Leggo! Beast. Ow! Stoppit! I'm going, ain't I?'

There was a full attendance on the pitch that afternoon. Most of the form enjoyed the game, but there were some who glowered as the Bounder strode around.

Later that afternoon, when Redwing told Smithy that he'd heard several discontented chaps muttering about him, the Bounder only laughed.

'So what? They voted me in, didn't they? They wanted success. That's why they got rid of Wharton. Well, they'll get it. I'm going to run the best team that Greyfriars has ever seen, and if I have to trample over a few slackers in order to do it, well, that's just their bad luck.'

'I hope it won't be yours, Smithy,' said Redwing, quietly.

Chapter 14

Stop it, Smithy!

'I wouldn't if I were you,' said Snoop.

'Nor me. You know what Smithy's temper's like. I wouldn't risk it,' agreed Stott.

Skinner scowled at his friends. It was Wednesday afternoon, and a half holiday. Most chaps were free until four o'clock when Smithy had fixed an extra games practice. Skinner, however, was an exception.

He had been booked for extra school, and from three to four o'clock he would be doing French for Monsieur Charpentier. Furthermore, he had been caught twisting the arm of a younger boy who had knocked his cap off, and Quelch had given him a hefty bunch of lines and warned him that he'd be whacked if he ever did it again.

Skinner was feeling particularly vindictive that afternoon. He didn't dare hit back at Monsieur Charpentier or Mr Quelch, but Smithy was a possible target. However, Snoop and Stott didn't take the same view.

'We'll never have a better chance,' said Skinner.

'I don't know,' said Snoop doubtfully. 'I don't think it's worth it.'

'You mean you haven't got the nerve,' sneered Skinner. 'What about you, Stott?'

'I dunno. Smithy's got a swollen head, but if he found out——'

'And he might,' said Snoop.

'What are you afraid of?' asked Skinner. 'Even if Smithy knew that we'd wrecked his study, what could he do?'

'Quite a lot,' said Snoop, grimly.

'Anyway, he's not going to find out,' argued Skinner. 'I've been looking out of the window. He's in the quad with Redwing.'

'Quelch might come up,' said Stott, nervously. 'You know he prowls round the studies now and again. He caught Smithy smoking only the other day, and whacked him.'

'Use your eyes, can't you?' snapped Skinner. 'He's in the quad too, marching up and down like some grenadier.'

'Um,' said Stott doubtfully.

'Haven't you got any guts? It's as safe as houses. No one's up here, and Smithy's been asking for it. He made us think that life was going to be easier with him in charge, and see what's happened. He's thrown his weight around ever since he got elected. He's worse than Wharton. He tricked us into voting for him, didn't he?'

'Well, yes, but——'

'If we're going to get our own back, now's the time. We can ship his study, and he'll never know who did it. There are plenty of others who might have done it. It won't take more than five minutes. As soon as we've finished, I'll shoot off to extra school and you can make yourselves scarce——'

'I'm making myself scarce right now,' said Stott, and he walked out of the study.

Skinner scowled after him, and then he turned to Snoop. 'Coming, Snoop?'

Snoop shook his head. 'I'm not putting my head into the lion's den,' he said firmly. 'If you do it, I hope you get away with it, but count me out.'

'Oh, go and play marbles!' snapped Skinner. 'That's all you're fit for,' and he left the study. He looked quickly up and down to make sure that no one else was about, and then he slipped quietly down the passage, and stopped outside the door of study no 4.

He hesitated for a moment. For all his talk, the last thing he wanted was trouble with Smithy, but it seemed safe enough. Vernon-Smith and Redwing were in the quad, and Quelch was strolling up and down the path beneath the study windows. At last, he made up his mind, pushed open the door, and slithered inside.

'Oh!' There was a sudden squeak. 'Oh, crumbs!'

'Oh!' gasped Skinner, completely taken aback.

He stared across the room at a fat figure who was straightening up from the cupboard, and twisting round to see who had come in.

'Bunter! You fat fool!' Skinner looked at the Owl angrily. It had never occurred to him that the study might be occupied by someone else.

'Apple crumble!' moaned Billy Bunter. 'I—I say, Skinner—Smithy ain't here. If—if you're looking for him, he—he's in the quad. Saw him there before I came up. Made sure—no, no that is, happened to look out of the window. Spotted him chatting to Redwing.'

Skinner thought quickly. He hadn't wanted anyone to know that he'd been there, and he was tempted to boot Bunter down the passage, but he resisted the impulse. There was another way of dealing with the fat man.

'I was going to speak to Smithy about games practice,' he said, casually. 'I'm in detention, and it's a bit much to have to get down to the field straight away. I wondered if he'd let me off.'

'Tee, hee, hee! You've got a hope!' tittered Bunter. 'Won't let anyone off. He's a rotten beast. I jolly well wish Wharton was still captain. He's a beast too, but he's not as beastly as Smithy.'

'Oh, so that's what you think?'

Bunter gave Skinner a fat wink. 'I say, Skinner. You're not as thick with Smithy as you used to be, are you? Why—why don't you have a go at his cake? There's lots and lots.'

He was holding a thick wedge in a fat paw, with crumbs spotting his blazer, and others littering the floor.

'You fat freak!' Skinner sounded disapproving but

actually he was delighted to see Smithy's cake disappearing down the path that led to Bunter's stomach. 'You're taking a chance. How do you know Smithy won't come up?'

'Told you,' mumbled Bunter, through a mouthful of cake. 'Looked out of the window. He's in the far corner of the quad. Smashing cake, this is. You can have——'

Skinner gave him a hard look. 'You pilfering porker! I've got a good mind to let him know what you've been up to,' and he walked out of the study, shutting the door behind him.

'I—I say, Skinner, old chap,' stammered Bunter. 'Don't—don't say nothing. I—I ain't had much. Don't—don't give a pal away.'

As soon as he was outside, Skinner sidled into the next study, and peeped through a crack in the door. As he expected, the Owl soon emerged, a large wedge of cake in either hand. He gave an anxious blink up and down the passage, and then rolled off at top speed towards the landing.

Skinner sighed with relief. Bunter wouldn't spill the beans if Smithy kicked up a row when he found his study shipped. It would mean confessing that he'd been there, and then the Bounder would know where his cake had gone.

He slipped into Smithy's study, shut the door, and risked a quick glance down into the quad. Vernon-Smith and Redwing could just be seen in the distance, and he could see the top of Quelch's head as he paced up and down beneath the window.

Satisfied, Skinner set to work. He piled books and papers into the hearth, and tipped ink over them. He opened a bottle of glue, dripped it over an expensive leather armchair and, using a piece of paper, spread it over the seat and arms. Grabbing the poker, he stuck it up the chimney, intending to rake down some soot and throw it about, but a sound made him stop.

Someone was pounding up the stairs.

A voice came from below. 'Smithy! Stop!'

Skinner went white. 'Oh!' he gasped, and stared round the room like a trapped animal. Almost without thinking, he backed into a corner, and crouched down behind a large wing-backed armchair. He was only just in time. The door was flung open, and the Bounder rushed into the study.

'Smithy!' Redwing was racing along the passage.

Skinner bit his lip, afraid that the Bounder would see the mess he had made, but obviously he had something else in mind. He heard the click of a door being opened, and then Vernon-Smith strode towards the window.

There was another crash, and Redwing hurtled in. 'Don't, Smithy!' he panted.

'Shut up!'

'You're a fool, Smithy!'

Skinner pricked up his ears, wondering what the Bounder was up to.

'I don't need your advice!'

'But——'

'Mind your own business!' The Bounder sounded as if he was in a towering rage. 'Leave me alone, you interfering idiot! I'm going to do it!'

'Oh, no you're not. You must be off your head, Smithy. If you shovel that onto Quelch, there'll be the biggest row ever heard in Greyfriars.'

'I'll do what I like.'

'Not if I have anything to do with it. Quelch will be so hopping mad——'

'Good! That's what I want. He whacked me for smoking——'

'But you asked for it,' pointed out Redwing. 'What did you expect him to do? Offer you a light? If you're caught——'

'Don't be a bigger fool than you can help,' sneered Smithy. 'He won't have the slightest idea where it came from. No one's going to see me tip a bag of flour out of the window——'

Skinner caught his breath. So that was what the Bounder was up to.

'But Smithy——' said Redwing.

'I've been waiting for a chance to use it. Well, now it's come. Quelch is still pounding his beat. It couldn't be better.'

'If you're caught——' said Redwing again.

The Bounder gave a confident laugh. 'Not a chance. Not a hope. That flour's been parked in the cupboard for over a week. I haven't been anywhere near the kitchens, have I? I'll clear off as soon as it's landed. I'll be far away by the time anyone gets here. No one's seen us come in. Quelch won't be able to pin it on me.'

'But it's a dirty, rotten trick——'

'Go and preach to someone else. You make me sick.'

'It's a filthy thing to do. You're form captain. You're supposed to have some sense of responsibility.'

'Rot!' snapped the Bounder.

'It's a mean thing to do.'

'I'll do what the hell I like!'

Redwing took a deep breath. 'Smithy, you can't! Quelch might——'

'He isn't going to know who did it,' said the Bounder impatiently, 'not unless your precious conscience gets the better of you. Now take your hand off me before I punch your head in. Quelch isn't going to be down there for ever. I'll never get another chance like this.'

'You're not getting it now.' Redwing sounded determined.

'Let go!' hissed Smithy.

'Not until you've put the flour back.'

'I'm warning you! I'll punch your head in,' said the Bounder, viciously.

There was a scuffle and then Smithy shouted, 'You fool! You've split the bag.'

'Good! Shove it back in the cupboard before it all trickles out.'

'No!'

'If you don't, I'll put my fist through it. You're not going to chuck it out of the window, and that's that.'

There was the sound of heavy breathing. 'You swine, Redwing!'

'All right. So I'm a swine.'

'It would have been a piece of cake.'

'Too bad.'

'You're a meddling fool!'

'Call me what you like, Smithy. Now, put it back before I burst it.'

Although Skinner couldn't see anything, he knew that the Bounder's eyes would be blazing with fury. However, it sounded as if Redwing had got the better of him for once.

Smithy moved away from the window. He tramped over to the cupboard, and something was slammed down. 'Now leave me alone,' he muttered.

'Coming?'

'No!'

'I shall stay here until you do.'

Feet moved towards the door. 'I won't forgive you for this, Redwing!'

'Don't be like that, Smithy. I only did it for you. I don't want you to get into a row.'

Skinner heard their footsteps disappearing down the passage, and cautiously he clambered from his hiding place, a cunning look on his face.

Chapter 15

Two Birds with One Stone

'Whew!' Skinner wiped the perspiration from his brow. He'd been lucky. Redwing and Smithy had been so busy struggling with each other that they hadn't even noticed what he'd done in the study.

He stood, staring at the specks of flour on the floor, and then walked quietly across to the window, and looked down. Quelch was still strolling up and down, blissfully unaware of his narrow escape.

Skinner's eyes glinted as he watched the mortar board bobbing along. Quelch had given him lines. He'd threatened him with a whacking. Like Smithy, he was longing to get his own back.

He gave a malicious smile. Maybe he could kill two birds with one stone. He'd got a score to settle with Smithy too. The Bounder had taken him for a ride over the election, and he hadn't forgiven him for that. If that bag of flour burst over Quelch's head, he wouldn't be suspected, but with any luck, Smithy would.

Skinner took a long, deep breath. For all his talk, he was cowardly rather than courageous. Usually his nerve wasn't equal to his malice, but in this case, he felt that he was safe enough.

He peered down once more, and at that moment, Quelch stopped pacing, and halted beneath the study window as Wingate came across the quad. Skinner backed. He had made up his mind. Swiftly, he crossed the room, removed the flour from the cupboard, and looked at the split in the bag. A tiny stream of white trickled out, powdering his sleeves with white and leaving a little trail on the carpet as he hurried towards the window.

Then he hesitated. The Bounder had nerve. If he

had been carrying out the operation, he would have aimed, watched it land accurately on its target, and then, looking perfectly composed, he would have sauntered away.

Skinner, however, lacked Smithy's nerve, and he was already frightened at his own intentions. For a moment, he was tempted to fling the flour across the room, and rush off, but he couldn't resist the idea of getting his own back on Smithy and Quelch at the same time.

He didn't dare to look out of the window again, but he knew exactly where Quelch was standing, for he could hear a faint murmur of voices. Taking a deep breath, Skinner dropped the bag of flour and then he turned and raced to the safety of his study.

The most important thing to do was to get every trace of flour from his clothing. If a grain was left, he felt sure that Quelch's gimlet eye would spot it. He ran breathlessly into study no 11, and kicked the door shut behind him.

There was a startled exclamation. 'Skinner!' Snoop stared blankly at him. 'What——?'

'Keep your voice down!' hissed Skinner.

'But what——?'

'Sh! Get me a clothes brush. Hurry up!' Skinner said.

Snoop stared at him in amazement. 'You're smothered in flour. It's all over you. What's happened?'

'Shut up!' said Skinner. 'Get a brush. Make it snappy.'

'Okay—but what's——?'

'Stop asking questions. I'll be for the high jump if I'm spotted looking like this. Where's the brush?'

'Can't see it,' said Snoop, peering in the table drawer.

Skinner elbowed him on one side, and rummaged in the drawer. 'Here it is, you fool. Brush me down,

Snoop. Don't just stand there gawping, like an idiot. Get moving. It'll be detention in a couple of minutes, and I can't go in with this stuff all over me.'

'All right.' Snoop grabbed the brush from Skinner's shaking hand, and set to work.

Skinner watched anxiously. 'There's some on my shoulder, isn't there? What about my back? Did I get any in my hair?' Gradually, as Snoop brushed vigorously, the flecks disappeared, and Skinner began to smirk. He'd get away with it, he knew he would.

Snoop stood back at last, and examined him carefully. 'That'll do,' he said, 'but what's it all about.' He eyed Skinner curiously. 'What have you been up to?'

Skinner laughed. 'You'll soon hear about it.'

'Come on. Out with it.'

'I've got my own back, that's what's happened,' he said, with a look of malicious satisfaction. 'Quelch is down in the quad looking a bit like a miller.'

'What's that?'

'I told you. Keep your voice down.' Skinner glanced down at himself again. 'Are you sure it's all off.'

'Yes, but——'

Skinner smirked. 'Listen. Keep it dark. Don't say a word to anyone about this—not even Stott.' He scanned his clothes, twisting rather like a cat chasing its tail to make sure that there were no tell-tale traces left.

'You really——?'

There was a chime from the clock tower. 'I'll have to get down.' Skinner threw the clothes brush to Snoop. 'I'm counting on you,' he said. 'If this gets around, I'll know why.'

'I shan't say a word.'

'You'd better not even breathe a syllable,' said Skinner.

'You don't have to worry, but—but—if Quelch got plastered with flour, there's going to be a terrific row.'

'So what?' said Skinner. 'I shall be in the clear. If anyone asks, you're going to say that we were together here until I went down to extra school, and that I wasn't out of your sight for a second. Not that you need worry. If anyone's suspected, it won't be me.'

'Then who?'

'Never you mind,' said Skinner. 'Now listen, I've got to get down to detention. All you've got to do is to keep your mouth shut.'

'Okay. You can count on me, but——'

Skinner didn't wait to hear the end of Snoop's sentence. He gave a last glance at his clothes, and left the study. He raced down the stairs just in time to join the small group of fellows who were also booked for extra school.

'Rotten being stuck in detention, isn't it?' said Smith. 'It's lucky old Sharpy hasn't got here yet. You've only just made it. Where were you? Out in the quad?'

'No,' replied Skinner, quickly. 'I was nattering away with Snoop in the study. I simply didn't notice the time.'

At that moment Monsieur Charpentier swept round the corner, and opened the door of the form room so that they could file in. Skinner looked as disgruntled as the rest as he settled down to work, but had Monsieur Charpentier been observing him, he might have wondered just why it was that he grinned from time to time. French verbs weren't often considered funny.

Chapter 16
By Whose Hand?

As Skinner was bolting into his study, there was a babble of voices in the quad.

'Oh, my hat!' exclaimed Bob Cherry.

'By gum!' breathed Johnny Bull.

The quad had been crowded with people sauntering in the bright, autumn sunshine. Quelch and Wingate had been standing beneath the study windows when a missile had whizzed down and had exploded on the ground. A fountain of something white and powdery had shot up into the air, and had drifted down again, some settling onto Quelch's gown, and some on Wingate's trousers and blazer as they had leaped backwards.

'Bless my soul!' exclaimed Quelch, looking astonished.

'What on earth—' said Wingate, and they watched the little cloud of white still rising into the air.

'Good gracious, Wingate! I believe it is flour!'

'You're right, sir. It's flour,' repeated Wingate. He watched a little ripple of it being blown along the ground by a gentle breeze.

Quelch stared as if he could hardly believe his eyes. 'Whatever has happened?'

'But—' Wingate stared blankly at his trousers and at Quelch's gown, and then he looked up at the Remove study windows. The flour must have come from there, but no one was to be seen.

'Upon my soul!' Quelch, still astounded, but sounding calmer. 'It must have been thrown from a window, Wingate. It couldn't have been dropped accidentally.'

'That's right, sir,' agreed Wingate.

'It might very well have landed right on top us us.'

'It very nearly did,' said Wingate.

A FOUNTAIN OF SOMETHING WHITE AND POWDERY HAD
SHOT UP INTO THE AIR . . .

'What stupid behaviour! Thoughtless and stupid! Only a—' Quelch broke off. His gimlet eyes glinted, and he compressed his lips as it occurred to him that the bag of flour might not have been carelessly tossed out of the window by a light-hearted boy. It had probably been intended for himself or for Wingate. 'Good heavens!' he said, and stared down, first at the bag and then, like Wingate, up at the windows. 'I don't think that it was an accident, Wingate.'

'Neither do I,' said the school captain.

'It was dropped intentionally.'

'Yes.'

Mr Quelch gave Wingate a grim smile. 'And do you think it was meant for you or for me, Wingate?'

'I really don't know,' Wingate replied.

'I have very little doubt about the matter.'

Although no one in the quad could hear what was said, they didn't think it was an accident either, and felt that it had been intended for Quelch.

'My Tuesday titfer!' breathed Bob. 'There's going to be big trouble over this. Look at our Henry. I don't think he's ever looked so furious before.'

'He's livid,' agreed Frank.

'He'll go on the rampage if he finds out who did it,' remarked Johnny.

'I rather think that our esteemed form master will eat whoever it was alive,' said Hurree Singh.

'Who would be potty enough to do it?' asked Harry.

'Oh, crumbs!' exclaimed Bob, as the memory of something flashed into his mind. 'You don't think——'

'What?' demanded Johnny.

'You don't think that that blundering fool Bunter could have had anything to do with it, do you?'

Harry looked at him enquiringly. 'Why pick on Bunter?'

'I caught him larking about with a bag of flour a few days ago. The idiot was trying to set a booby-trap for

Smithy. Could he have been half-witted enough——?'

'Never!' said Johnny bluntly. 'Not our Bunter. He wouldn't have the nerve.'

'I doubt whether our fat friend could have done it,' said Hurree. 'If he had aimed for Quelch, it would have landed miles away. He's not the best shot in the Remove.'

'But he did have a bag of flour,' persisted Bob. 'I bet he filched it from the kitchens, and he wouldn't have put it back again. No one else stores flour in his study.'

'I wonder where he is,' Frank said.

'Probably frowsting over the fire in the Rag,' grunted Johnny. 'He doesn't get on too well with fresh air.'

'Or soap and water, come to that,' added Hurree.

'Let's go and find out,' suggested Bob.

'Yes, let's,' agreed Frank, leading the way indoors.

As they left the quad, more and more people crowded in as the news spread. Prout, Capper, Hacker, and other masters appeared, and prefects turned up to see if they could help. There was a lot of noise and excitement, all directed at Quelch and Wingate. Quelch, his face grim and set, was dusting the flour from his gown. Wingate was gazing up at the windows again, his focused on study no 4, the only room with an open window.

The Famous Five edged their way through the crowd and made their way into the House, looking for the fat Owl. Johnny's prediction proved to be right. He was in the common room, sitting in front of the fire.

'I say, you fellows!' he squeaked, as they hurried in, and he gave them a friendly blink through his big, round specs.

'Hallo, hallo, hallo, fat man. So this is where you've been hanging out.'

'Eh?' Billy Bunter blinked at Bob Cherry in sur-prise. 'Course I'm here. Not going out till I have to.'

'You'll have to soon,' said Frank. 'Time's getting on. We're due for soccer.'

'Tain't fair,' grumbled Billy Bunter. 'Why should we have an extra practice? Tain't compulsory. I jolly well don't see why we should turn out. You back me up, you chaps. I—I don't mind if Johnny tells Smithy where he gets off. Don't want all the limelight, you know. What about that?'

'You're wrong. It is compulsory,' said Bob. 'Smithy told Wingate that we needed more practice, and so Wingate fixed it.

'Rotten beast!' moaned the Owl.

'How long have you been here, Bunter?' asked Harry. He had already looked at Bunter's clothes. Although there were no traces of flour on him, there were quite a lot of crumbs and splashes of gravy.

'Ever—ever since lunch,' Bunter said, giving him an uneasy blink. 'Didn't do very well,' he added peevishly. 'Only three goes at baked ham roll and four at apple tart. Getting mean about grub, they are. Not so long ago I could have counted on——'

'Have you been up to the studies?'

'Me? Not likely,' said Bunter. 'Never went to Smithy's study if that's what you're on about. No reason. Never knew he'd got a cake. Wouldn't have wanted it, not from that beast, even though it was a chocolate one.'

'Listen, pork pie!' shouted Bob. 'Give us a straight answer. When were you in Smithy's study?'

'But—but I told you I never was,' hooted Bunter. 'Never did. Didn't know there were walnuts on top of it.'

Bob Cherry seized the fat Owl's collar. 'I'm going to shake the truth out of you!'

'Stoppit, you great oaf! Gimme a chance. Was going to say. I—that is, about half an hour ago, except that I wasn't there.'

As Bob let go, Harry said, 'Then you didn't chuck a

bag of flour out of the window?'

Bunter's eyes bulged, and he almost managed to struggle into an upright position. 'What? Why?'

'I saw you with a bag of flour last week,' said Bob Cherry. 'You were going to use it on Smithy, but you didn't set up that booby-trap, did you? What happened to the flour?'

'I never done nothing with it,' said Bunter indignantly. 'Would have, but you were a rotten mean beast, Cherry. You could have given me a hand.'

'What did you do with it?' asked Harry, patiently.

'Nothing. That rotter Smithy took it off me. He was going to split it over my head except that Redwing wouldn't let him.'

'So Smithy had it!' exclaimed Harry.

'Did he hang on to it?' asked Frank.

'Yes, he jolly well did. I spotted it in his study cupboard when I found that cake—that is, when I didn't find the cake. I—I say, if Smithy cuts up rough about it, you'll remember that I wasn't there, won't you. It—it wasn't me who sampled it, and——'

'You fathead!'

'You greedy gannet!'

'Oh, I say, Nugent! That's going a bit far,' said Bunter, as the Famous Five walked out of the Rag.

'I guess he's in the clear,' said Frank.

'I—I say,' shouted Bunter, just as Harry was closing the door. 'About that extra practice. Are you going to tell Smithy what you think of him?'

'We'll leave it to you,' Johnny yelled back.

'Beast!' Bunter returned to his armchair.

The Famous Five strolled out into the quad again. The excitement had died down, and most of the flour had drifted away.

'It sounds as if it was Smithy,' said Bob, in a low voice. 'He wouldn't have kept that bag of flour for nothing. He must have intended to use it.'

Others, it seemed had come to the same conclusion.

It wasn't long before they learned that the prefects were out in strength, looking for him.

Chapter 17

Smithy is Wanted

'Smithy!' panted Redwing, relieved at finding him.

After their scuffle in study no 4, Smithy had flung out of the House in a savage temper, probably more angry and exasperated with his friend than he would have been with an enemy.

He was sitting in a secluded corner of the cloisters, a cigarette in his hand, and an expression of bitter anger and resentment on his face. He gave Redwing a black scowl. 'What do you want?'

'I've been hunting all over the place for you.'

'Why? I don't want to talk to you.'

'For goodness sake, Smithy,' said Redwing. 'Don't——'

'Why don't you clear off?'

'Stub out that cigarette,' said Redwing, urgently. 'You don't want to be found smoking on top of everything else. The prefects are looking for you.'

'For me?' repeated Smithy, astonished. 'What for?'

'Can't you guess?'

'How can I? I haven't done anything. You didn't give me a chance, but I'll get my own back on Quelch if it's the last thing I do.' He gave Redwing a scornful look. 'I'll make sure you're not around next time.'

'Why lie to me, Smithy? They're not looking for you for nothing. Anyway, you weren't quite as clever as you thought you were. You missed Quelch. The bag burst at his feet.'

'Bag? I didn't do anything with it. I left it in the study cupboard. You saw me put it there.'

'You mean you didn't chuck it out of the window?'

Smithy took a deep breath. 'Do you mean that somebody else did?'

'Yes, but if it wasn't you——'

'I've said so, haven't I? What happened?'

'Like I said. It almost landed on Quelch's nut when he was talking to Wingate.'

Vernon-Smith whistled. 'Phew!' He ground out the stub of his cigarette. 'Let's get it straight. The flour was dropped——'

'Yes, from one of the study windows.'

'Well, it had nothing to do with me.' The Bounder's eyes glinted as he saw the doubt in Redwing's face. 'Don't be such a fool! You know perfectly well that I put it back, and then you followed me downstairs and saw me go out.'

Redwing looked the Bounder straight in the eye. 'And you didn't go back later on?'

'No.'

'And you've been here ever since?'

'That's right.' The Bounder gave him a malevolent look. 'You don't believe me, do you? You're not much of a friend. You can clear off. Leave me alone.'

'Oh, come on, Smithy,' said Redwing. 'Be reasonable. Of course I believe you since you say so——'

'Thanks,' said the Bounder, sarcastically.

'But you can see how suspicious it looked. I had a job to stop you in the first place, and then I lost sight of you. I didn't know where you were. But listen, if it wasn't you——'

'I've told you!' said Smithy, irritably. 'I don't know anything about it. For all I know, that flour's still in the cupboard. I came straight out here to have a fag. I was hot under the collar. I wanted to cool off. I'd come close to punching your silly head and——'

'Can't you forget that? The point is, Quelch must think that it's you. That's why the prefects——'

'Why should he? He's just picked on me. It's the

same old story. Give a dog a bad name——'

'Okay, okay. The thing is, as soon as I heard Gwynne and Loder asking if anyone had seen you, I came looking for you. I wanted to tip you off. I thought that if you were keeping out of sight——'

The Bounder gave a harsh laugh. 'Thanks,' he said, sourly. 'I'm glad to know what you think of me. You thought that I was skulking in a corner, didn't you?'

'No, I didn't. I thought it would just be better if you showed up. I admit that I thought you did it, but——'

'As it happens, I didn't, but I wonder who it was. He must have been a rotten shot. Quelch was a sitting duck.'

'If Quelch finds out who it was, there'll be real trouble. It could come to a sacking. But I wonder why Quelch thought you were involved.'

'He can think what he likes,' said the Bounder, carelessly. 'Quelch can't get me for it. I wasn't around.'

They both looked up at the sound of heavy footsteps, and Loder came round the corner. 'What are you doing here, Vernon-Smith?' he demanded. 'We've been looking for you.'

'What do you want me for?' asked the Bounder, coolly. 'Anyway, why shouldn't I be here? The cloisters aren't out of bounds, are they?'

'Don't be so cheeky!' said Loder, sharply. 'Quelch wants you, and he wants you now. Come on. You too, Redwing. You share his study, don't you?'

'Yes, Loder,' replied Redwing, quietly.

The Bounder gave Loder an insolent look. 'And what an I supposed to have done?'

'You mean you want me to tell you?'

'That's right.'

Loder gave a short laugh. 'I must say you've got a nerve, Vernon-Smith. You threw the flour out of the window, didn't you?'

'No,' said Smithy, flatly.

'Oh, so it's news to you?'

'Not exactly,' said the Bounder, calmly. 'It was news about five minutes ago when Redwing told me about it.'

Loder looked at him in disbelief. 'You tell Quelch that! Come on. Get moving.'

The prefect turned, and walked away, the juniors following. The Bounder was quite cool. He hadn't been anywhere near the quad at the time, and so he saw no reason for alarm.

Redwing, on the other hand, was troubled. He was sure that Smithy had told him the truth, but Quelch wouldn't have wanted to see him for nothing.

A lot of fellows watched as they walked across the quad, aware that Smithy was under suspicion.

'I say,' squeaked Bunter, in a state of high excitement. 'They've got Smithy at last. Serve him right, the beast.'

Squiff confronted the Bounder. 'You're rock bottom!' he said, bluntly. 'A fine thing for our form captain to do. Quelch might be a pain in the neck, but it's a lousy trick to smother him with flour like that.'

The Bounder scowled. 'It's nothing to do with me!' he snapped.

'Oh, yes?' Squiff didn't sound convinced.

There was a chuckle from the fat Owl. 'Hee, hee, hee! Then what did you keep that bag of flour in the cupboard for?'

Smithy swung round, and gave Bunter a look of blistering hatred. 'Why can't you keep your big mouth shut, you fat bladder of lard?' He looked at Loder, wondering if he had heard.

'That's right!' said Bob Cherry. 'Whatever he's done, it's nothing to do with you. You keep quiet!'

'Thanks,' said the Bounder, 'but I haven't done anything, Cherry.'

'Not much!' grunted Johnny Bull.

Loder turned back. 'What are you dragging your

feet for, Vernon-Smith? Quelch's temper won't improve if he's kept waiting.'

'Let's move,' muttered Redwing.

The Bounder trailed after Loder, well aware that no one believed in his innocence.

Chapter 18

Guilty!

There was a grim and unyielding look on the face of Mr Quelch as he sat at his desk regarding the two juniors who had been marched in by Loder. Although he scrutinised both, his attention was concentrated on Vernon-Smith.

Smithy hadn't the slightest idea of why Quelch had picked on him, but he felt that he had already been convicted, and his face became sullen. He was also pretty sure that Redwing was there only because they shared a study. Quelch wouldn't suspect anyone so quiet and steady.

'Thank you, Loder,' said Quelch, and waited until the prefect had left the room. He rested his hands on the desk, and spoke to Smithy. 'I am quite sure,' he said, 'that you know what happened a short time ago.'

'Yes, sir,' replied Smithy, promptly. 'Redwing told me about a quarter of an hour ago.'

Quelch's eyebrows lifted a little. 'You knew nothing until Redwing told you?'

'No, sir.'

'And where were you when he told you of the incident?'

'I was in the cloisters, Mr Quelch.'

'Was anyone with you?'

'No, I was alone, sir.'

Quelch's eyes narrowed. 'That does not surprise me. Now, Vernon-Smith, I want the truth. Did you have anything to do with that disgraceful incident?'

'No,' said the Bounder, steadily. 'Nothing at all.'

'Very well. Quelch folded his hands, and leaned forward. 'I must tell you that the bag of flour was thrown from your study window. There is no doubt about it.'

Smithy looked astonished. 'But how do you know, sir? It could have been thrown from any of the windows.'

'No.' Mr Quelch shook his head. 'Yours was the only open window——'

'But a window could have been closed after the flour had been thrown.'

'That is true, but there is something else. I have been into every study. A considerable amount of flour has been spilled on your carpet. There isn't a trace of it anywhere else.'

Smithy looked at Redwing. He was staggered at this piece of news. It was true that the bag had been split during their tussle, but only a few grains could have trickled out.

'I simply don't understand, sir,' he said, 'but I—I suppose anyone could have gone into my study.'

'Did you not know that there was a bag of flour in your study cupboard?'

The Bounder hesitated before answering. He wasn't guilty, but things were beginning to look black.

'I should tell you, Vernon-Smith,' said Mr Quelch, severely, 'that the plainest possible traces have been found there. I think that the bag had been damaged, and some of it had been spilled onto the shelf.'

The Bounder took a deep breath. 'Yes, Mr Quelch,' he said. 'There was a bag of flour there.'

'Why was it there?'

'But I didn't throw it from the window. Truly, Mr Quelch, I had no idea of what had happened until Redwing told me.'

Mr Quelch gave him a keen look. 'You have not

answered my question. I asked what a bag of flour was doing in your cupboard.'

'I—that is, someone was going to play a trick on me. I took it away from him.'

'And when was this?'

'One day last week. Redwing was there.'

'Yes, that's right,' said Redwing.

'Very well. I will accept that, but it only explains how it came into your possession. It does not explain why you kept it there. What was your intention?'

'There wasn't any reason, sir. I simply put it away and forgot all about it.'

Redwing flushed. The Bounder was telling an outright lie.

Mr Quelch's face became even grimmer. 'I want you to think before you answer me, Vernon-Smith. Are you telling me that you did not remove the bag from the cupboard?'

'I didn't touch it,' said the Bounder, emphatically.

A look of distaste crossed Quelch's face, and at that moment, Smithy realised that somehow or other his form master knew that he had been lying.

'Upon my word! So you didn't touch the bag of flour this afternoon?' As the Bounder remained silent, Quelch went on, 'Then perhaps you will explain why there are specks of flour on your sleeves.'

'Oh!' Smithy looked down. He had brushed himself after the struggle with Redwing, but he hadn't taken a great deal of trouble over it. After all, it hadn't seemed important.

Redwing's heart sank. If Smithy had told the truth, there was a chance he might had been believed, but now that he had been caught out in a lie, Quelch would find it hard to be convinced by anything else that he might say.

'Well?' rapped Quelch. 'What have you to say?'

'I—I—' stammered Smithy.

'Are you going to persist in your denial, Vernon-

Smith?'

'No, sir,' muttered the Bounder. 'But—but I didn't throw it from the window, Mr Quelch. Really I didn't. I admit that I took it from the cupboard, but I put it back, I didn't do anything with it. I—I was going to use it, but Redwing persuaded me not to.'

As Mr Quelch raised his hand, the Bounder fell silent. 'You have already lied. I trust you are not lying again.' He turned his attention to Redwing. 'What happened, Redwing?'

'That is what happened, sir. He did return the flour to the cupboard. I watched him do it, and then I followed him from the room.'

Mr Quelch fixed his gimlet eyes on the Bounder again. 'I think I can guess what you intended to do, Vernon-Smith. Now Redwing, I already know that he was alone in the cloisters. Am I to take it that you did not remain with him?'

Redwing looked first at the Bounder, and then at his form master. If only Smithy hadn't flung off in such a filthy temper, he might have been able to prove his innocence.

'Now come along, Redwing. I am waiting for an answer.'

'No, sir,' said Redwing, reluctantly. 'I lost sight of him.'

'I see. I think we have got to the bottom of the matter. You may go, Redwing.'

Redwing turned and walked out, miserably aware that Smithy was in deep trouble.

Vernon-Smith remained silent. He knew that it was hopeless to try and persuade Quelch that he was innocent. He seldom regretted anything that he said or did, but he did regret lying this time.

'I do not know, and nor do I want to know whether you intended to hit Wingate or myself with that bag of flour. If it had landed on its target, I should have taken you straight to Dr Locke. As it is, you will spend every half holiday in detention for the rest of the term. However, there is another matter that I must deal with. You have lied, and I shall cane for you for that.'

A little later, the Bounder, white-faced, left Quelch's study feeling savage and sullen. Tom Redwing was waiting anxiously around the corner for him, but Smithy brushed roughly past him, and tramped out into the quad.

Chapter 19

Vernon-Smith Wants to Know

'Wharton!' said the Bounder.

Harry Wharton and Frank Nugent looked up. They were in their study sorting out their books for prep. Smithy's face was flushed with anger, and Frank wondered if he was spoiling for a fight.

'Well, what is it?' asked Harry.

'I want a word with you.'

'Have two if you like.' Harry's manner was polite but indifferent.

The Bounder walked into the study, and leaned against the wall, his eyes on Harry. 'I expect you're as pleased as punch about all of this,' he said, bitterly.

'At all of what?'

'You know what I'm talking about. You must have felt as sick as a dog when I became form captain, and you were left out in the cold.'

'You can think what you like,' Harry said, casually.

'I know how you feel.'

'Do you?'

'Yes.'

Harry shrugged. 'I made a mistake. You made the most of it. I'm not blaming you for my mistakes.'

'So you admit that you made them?' sneered Smithy. 'That's a change.'

96

'Why not? We all make mistakes at times,' said Harry, carelessly. 'I hear you made a gigantic one this afternoon.'

The Bounder's face became gloomier. 'That's why I'm here. I'm in detention for the rest of the term.'

'I know.'

'I'm not going to be able to play in any of the matches.'

'I know.' Harry flicked open a book. 'Is there anything else?'

The Bounder didn't move. 'I bet you're laughing up your sleeve.'

'Yes?' Harry's cool air infuriated the Bounder. 'Is that what you came to say?'

'I want to know if you've got any idea of who chucked that flour out of the window.'

Both Frank and Harry stared at the Bounder.

'Yes,' said Harry, at last.

'Who?' demanded the Bounder.

Harry's eyes flickered up and down him. 'You,' he said.

Smithy breathed hard. 'Would it do any good if I told you that it wasn't me?'

·'Not much.'

'Well, I'm telling you just the same.' Smithy's expression grew blacker. Clearly, neither of them believed him. 'I'll tell you exactly what happened.'

'Don't bother. I think we can guess.'

'Listen——'

Harry sighed. 'All right, but don't overdo it, Smithy. We all know that you'd got a bag of flour stashed away, and everyone knows that it was dropped from your window. Why had you hung onto it? You weren't thinking of taking up cooking, were you?'

'I'm not denying that I was keeping it for Quelch,' said Smithy, quickly. 'I meant to do it. I would have, if Redwing hadn't stopped me, but I swear that I put it back. I didn't see it after that. I went out of the study with Redwing, and I didn't return.' There was silence, and the Bounder looked from one to the other. 'You don't believe me, do you?' he said.

'Does Quelch?' asked Frank.

'You know he doesn't. Do you?'

Frank looked at him. 'No.'

'But I'm not lying. Somebody else went into my study. I want to know who it was. Do you know anything about it, Wharton?'

'Me? Of course not. Why should I?'

'Isn't it obvious?' asked Smithy. 'I'm not going to be able to play in matches because of this. I reckon that it was a plot. Those traces of flour were deliberately left in my study to make me look guilty, and it worked only too well.' He paused. 'I've heard quite a lot of chaps say that you'll have to captain the team if I can't.'

Frank Nugent turned on Smithy. 'You've got a twisted mind, Vernon-Smith. Harry wouldn't——'

'Okay,' said the Bounder, hastily. 'Maybe I put it badly.'

'You can say that again.'

'I was just stating the facts. I want to find out who set me up. Someone will benefit if I'm stuck in detention, and that someone is——'

'Get out of this study!' yelled Frank.

'But you can't deny that Wharton——'

'I told you to get out!' shouted Frank.

'Don't get steamed up about it, Frank,' said Harry Wharton, calmly. 'Let him get it out of his system.' He smiled scornfully at Smithy. 'Keep going. Let's see where we've got to. You were saying that you didn't do it, and you've decided that it must have been me because I want to captain the team.'

'I haven't said that.'

'Not in so many words,' said Frank.

'All I've said is that I'm innocent. And I'm telling you something else. I'm going to find out who it was before the Rookwood match next Wednesday.'

'You listen to me, Smithy! You're barking up the wrong tree. As it happens, Harry was in the quad with the rest of us when that bag burst on the ground. There were probably a couple of dozen guys who saw us there. Of course,' Frank went on, sarcastically, 'we might all have been in the plot.'

For a moment, the Bounder was silenced. Suspicious though he was, he accepted the fact that Harry couldn't have had anything to do with it, and deep down, he knew that he wasn't capable of doing anything so underhand.

'But it's worked out nicely for you,' he said, bitterly. 'You'll come off best unless I can find out who did it. I—I suppose I knew that you didn't, but it occurred to me that one of your friends——'

'Thanks very much,' said Harry, contemptuously, 'but as it happens, I don't have friends like yours.'

'So you've no idea of who it could have been?'

'If it wasn't you, no!'

The Bounder turned to Frank. 'And you don't know either?'

Frank shrugged his shoulders. 'You want to see who did it?'

'Of course I do,' said Smithy, vehemently.

'There's a looking glass here.'

'And what do you mean by that?' demanded the Bounder, hotly.

'Go and have a look. You'll see for yourself who it was.'

Smithy clenched his fists so hard that his knuckles went white. 'You rotten swine, Nugent!'

Harry gave a little laugh. 'You're wasting your time here, Vernon-Smith. Try the other studies. See if anyone else can help you. If you're telling the truth, then I hope you nail the guy. I'm sorry, but I can't help.'

'But it suits your book, doesn't it?' said Smithy sullenly.

'As it happens, I haven't got a book, but you can believe what you like. Now, would you mind clearing out? Frank and I want to get on with our prep.'

The Bounder threw a black look at Harry, and tramped out of the room.

'I wonder,' murmured Harry. 'I just wonder who did it.'

'Don't waste your time,' said Frank, positively. 'It was Smithy, all right.'

'It could have been, but he was serious when he hinted that it was me. I just wonder if someone else was gunning for him. If that's the case, then he's had a raw deal.'

'Serve him right,' grunted Frank.

Chapter 20

Give Smithy a Chance!

'Forget it, Smithy,' said Redwing mildly.

'Forget it! How can I?' snapped the Bounder.

It was just before lunch on Saturday morning, and the two were in their study. In spite of his enquiries, Vernon-Smith still hadn't got any further in his search for the culprit.

Redwing looked weary. The Bounder had been going on about it for the last half hour. 'You might as well give up,' he said. 'No one saw anyone go up to the studies.'

'Reddy,' said the Bounder, seriously. 'I've got to get this sorted out. One or two chaps have been saying it was a mistake to let Wharton resign. If I can't play, he'll have to take over as captain. I'll lose everything I've gained, and all because some dirty rotter had it in for me.' As Redwing remained silent, the Bounder gave him a suspicious glance. 'You do believe me, don't you?'

Redwing sighed. 'I've told you I do, but I'm about the only guy who does.'

'It makes me sick. If Wharton's to act as captain, he might as well be the captain. It's turned out nicely for him, hasn't it? I can't get over it.'

'Then you'd better,' said Redwing sharply. 'You know Wharton better than that. He's got his faults, but you know that he wouldn't play a dirty trick on anyone.'

The Bounder frowned. 'I know,' he said. 'I don't suspect him, but someone else might have wanted to help him. It's either that, or it's someone who's got a down on me.'

'Or both,' added Redwing.

Smithy knitted his brow. 'What about Toddy? The only reason I got more votes that him was because Wharton didn't vote.'

'Toddy!' Redwing was appalled. 'He'd never do anything like that. Anyway, if he's got a down on someone, it would be Wharton, not you.'

'Well, who was it?' demanded Smithy.

'It's more likely to be someone who wanted you to get in trouble,' said Redwing, slowly. 'There was all that gum and ink spread around. It wasn't Wharton, and Toddy's out of the running, but there are others. You've needled a lot of chaps.'

'Okay, okay. There's no need to go on about it, but whoever it was, I'll get him soon or later. I'll make him wish that he'd never been born, the dirty rat!' Smithy smacked a fist into the palm of his other hand. 'Who was it?' he said again.

'I haven't a clue,' said Redwing, wearily.

'I must find out!' said the Bounder, passionately. 'I must. There's the Rookwood match coming up, and we've got a good chance of winning. If we do, then I'll be all right. Chaps who are still on Wharton's side will stop muttering if we win. I'll tell you one thing, Reddy. I'm leading that team out at Rookwood, detention or no detention. I just don't care!'

Redwing stared. 'But Smithy!' he exclaimed. 'You can't! You can't flout Quelch like that!'

'That's what you think.'

'But Smithy, you wouldn't get away with it. If you didn't turn up for detention, Quelch would soon hear about it, and he'd know why. He'd ring up, and get you sent back. It's no good. You'll just have to take your medicine.'

'But it isn't mine!' shouted Smithy. 'It isn't fair. I'm booked for extra school for the rest of the term for something I didn't do. It isn't fair.'

Redwing sighed as he looked at Smithy's angry face. 'Come on, Smithy,' he said. 'It'll be lunch soon. I don't want to be late. We've got the match against the fourth this afternoon and—' He stopped, remembering that the Bounder wouldn't be playing. 'Sorry, Smithy.'

Vernon-Smith's face grew blacker. 'You're only playing against Dabney's crew,' he said. 'It's hardly worth turning out.'

'It'll give the team a bit of a practice before the Rookwood game,' said Redwing, quietly.

'I'm getting there by hook or by crook,' Smithy muttered, as they made their way downstairs.

After lunch, most of the chaps went outside, but the Famous Five went into the Rag and stood at the open window. It was a fine day with a gentle breeze, and practically everyone looked cheerful as they stood chatting in the sunny quad.

Bob pointed to an exception. 'Think he's getting a kick out of life?' he asked, as Smithy walked moodily round the quad, a frown on his face.

'He looks as if life is giving him a kick in the teeth,' observed Hurree Singh.

'What a captain! Stuck in detention while his

team's playing!' Johnny sounded disgusted.

'That's Smithy all over,' said Frank.

Harry didn't speak, but he looked at Smithy, and felt a twinge of sympathy. It must be hard to be stuck in extra school during the first match of his new career. What was more, he now had a feeling that the Bounder was innocent.

'He'll have to watch out,' remarked Bob. 'Several blokes have already told him that he ought to resign.'

'He'll never do that,' said Johnny.

'He might be chucked out,' Frank said.

'Squiff said that he'd have punched Smithy's head in if he'd known what was going to happen. I say, Harry, Toddy was saying only last night that if there was another election, he wouldn't stand against you.' Bob looked eagerly at Harry. 'You'd be home and dry.'

Harry shook his head. 'Smithy hasn't had a chance yet.'

'But he has. He's had it, and he's thrown it away. You got chucked out because you wouldn't put him in the team, but now he's put himself out of the team.'

'If you hadn't been so obstinate, you'd still be captain,' said Johnny Bull, bluntly.

Harry gave him a faint smile. 'Thanks.'

'Take it easy, Johnny,' murmured Frank. 'We've been over all that before.'

'Why shouldn't I say it?' demanded Johnny Bull. 'That's what everyone thinks. There's no point in beating about the bush. Harry was a pig-headed——'

'Shut up all the same.'

Harry smiled faintly. 'I've thought quite a lot about it. I was right to start with, but Smithy got under my skin. Oh well, I asked for it, and I got it.'

'Glad you've come to your senses at last,' said Johnny. 'So you'd play Smithy if you had your chance all over again?'

'Yep.'

'With any luck, you'll soon be captain again,' Bob pointed out.

'He's got to have his chance,' repeated Harry. 'He's captain whether we like it or not.'

'We don't want someone who carries on like that,' said Johnny.

'I'm not so sure that it was Smithy,' said Harry, slowly. 'He's sworn that he didn't——'

'And what does that mean? He'd got the flour and he meant to use it on Quelch. He would have done if Reddy hadn't stopped him. I bet he nipped back——'

'I know he could have done, but——'

'Hallo, hallo, hallo! What are you after?' demanded Bob, as a small crowd appeared at the window.

'We want to speak to you, Wharton,' said Squiff.

'What is it this time? Not another ultimatum?'

There was an embarrassed silence. 'Never mind that,' said Peter, hastily. 'Look here——'

'It's this,' began Tom Brown.

Squiff cut across him. 'It's about soccer,' he explained. 'We can't let Smithy carry on, now that he's made such a fool of himself. You'll have to act as captain this afternoon, and there's Rookwood next week.'

'Hold on,' said Harry. 'If I'm picked, I'll play on Wednesday, that's all. Smithy's captain——'

'I know, but——'

'It's up to you to back up the chap you voted in.'

'But we wouldn't have, not if we'd known what he was going to do.'

'He's an idiot!' said Squiff. 'He's got to go, and that's all there is to it.'

'It's nothing to do with me,' said Harry quietly, 'but I think you should give him a chance.'

'Oh!' said Squiff, taken aback.

'What? Put up with someone who's played a dirty trick on Quelch!' exclaimed Toddy.

'Smithy says that he didn't do it, and I believe him.'

'Rot!'

'Rubbish!'

'You must be joking!'

Bob Cherry looked meaningly at his friends. 'Smithy would have taken a rather different line, Harry, if he'd been in your shoes.'

'He would if the truth were known,' Harry said. 'Maybe the chap who did it will have a twinge of conscience and own up.' He turned his back on the crowd at the window, and the fellows looked uncertainly at each other before straggling away.

Bob Cherry looked meaningly at his friends. 'Smithy would have taken a rather different line, Harry, if he'd been in your shoes.'

Harry turned round. 'I'm not Smithy,' he said, quietly.

The Bounder came up to the window, and leaned his elbows on the sill. 'Wharton!' He stared curiously at Harry. 'I couldn't help hearing what was said. I don't know what your game is, but——'

'I don't suppose you do.'

'What do you mean?'

'Work it out for yourself,' Harry said, casually.

The Bounder frowned. Bob had been right. If their positions had been reversed, he would have made the most of it, so he found it hard to believe that Harry had been sincere.

'What I really came to say to you was that you'll have to take over as captain this afternoon.' The Bounder sounded depressed. 'And if I can't go to Rookwood——'

'You might with a bit of luck,' said Harry. 'There's always the chance that the chap who bagged Quelch with that flour will own up.'

'What a hope!'

'If he's got a spark of decency——'

'If he had, he wouldn't have landed me in the mire in the first place.'

As the Bounder spoke, the clock chimed, and the Bounder scowled as he made his way into extra school.

Chapter 21

The Spider and the Fly

'Bunter!'

'Beast!'

It was tea time on Monday afternoon, and Billy Bunter was lingering near the door of study no 4 when Vernon-Smith came up. Bunter was hungry in spite of the fact that he and Toddy and Tom Dutton had already had an early tea. In Bunter's mind, bread and butter, jam, and a bun weren't much to write home about, and he was sadly conscious of the fact that Toddy and Dutton had eaten their share of what was going, in spite of the fact that he could, and willingly would have demolished the lot.

So he had rolled hopefully up the corridor to Lord Mauleverer, only to find that no one was at home and that he had, for once, locked his cupboard. Feeling a bit like a lion deprived of his prey, the fat Owl had rolled down the passage again, and had found Mauly having tea with the Famous Five. Although there wasn't much room, he'd been prepared to squeeze in, but a football boot whizzing across the room had suggested that he wasn't welcome.

And that was why William George was standing outside the Bounder's study, blinking anxiously at the door, wondering whether to risk a raid on Smithy's well-stocked cupboard or whether to make do with a second, and to his mind, frugal tea in the dining room.

The Owl blinked morosely at Smithy as he strolled towards his study. His feelings about the Bounder had see-sawed of late. A dictionary thudding on his fat chin had turned him into a resentful opponent. A marvellous spread had made him an enthusiastic supporter, but then Smithy had revealed himself as an oppressive tyrant, a captain who cared so little for his troops that he even drove sick men onto his parade ground, so to speak.

Billy Bunter's loathing for the Bounder was now almost as great as his loathing for lessons. It was true that a good spread would have brought him back onto Smithy's side again, but since a spread seemed most unlikely, he just gave a resentful blink, and said again, 'Beast!'

To his surprise, the Bounder gave him a friendly nod. 'I've been looking for you, Bunter. Had any tea?'

'Oh! Eh? Yes! That is, no. What I mean is——'

'What about having it with me?'

Billy Bunter could hardly believe his fat ears. He wondered what had come over Smithy, but he didn't spend much time wondering. It wasn't all that important. Tea was what mattered. He beamed at the Bounder. 'I—I say, Smithy, that's decent of you.'

'Trot in,' said Smithy, hospitably, and opened the door.

Bunter cantered in, almost whinnying with pleasure. As he happily helped to put food on the table, he thought that life was odd. Not long ago, he had been contemplating a raid on those good things, and now he was actually being asked to dispose of them.

It was one of the best teas that he could ever remember, and Smithy was at his most affable, pressing the fat Owl to help himself to yet more ham and eggs, chocolate cake, jam tarts, and meringues.

'Isn't Redwing coming?' asked Billy Bunter, at last. Having eaten enough for three or four starving men, he had time to remember his existence.

Smithy shook his head. 'No, he's having tea with Ogilvy,' but he didn't mention the fact that he had

'AND WHAT ABOUT THE JAM TARTS?'

asked Redwing to keep out of the way.

'All the more for us. I say, Smithy, this is a jolly good cake. Nearly as good as the ones we get at Bunter Court. There ain't much left. Would it help if I finished it off? Don't want bits and pieces left, do you?'

'Help yourself,' said Smithy.

'And what about the jam tarts? You can't do much with four, can you?'

'Not much,' agreed the Bounder, watching two fat paws grabbing them.

A little later, a happy and sticky Owl pushed his chair back. 'I—I say, Smithy, old chap. You just wait till my postal order comes. I'll stand you a spread. Some chaps just take, take, take. I'm not like that. We Bunters have got a sense of obligation. You just wait——'

'Oh, I know,' said Smithy, trying to keep a straight face. 'But you mustn't let it bother you. You must come again.'

'Gosh!' gasped Bunter. 'I—I say——'

'Come as often as you like. It'll be a pleasure.'

The Owl blinked with delight, and visions of unlimited teas floated before his dazzled eyes. 'Oh, I say!'

'But there is something you can do for me,' added the Bounder, casually.

It had crossed Bunter's mind that Smithy hadn't asked him for nothing, although he hadn't the remotest idea of what it could be. Actually, he felt that it didn't matter what it was as long as Smithy went on being so hospitable.

'Anything you like!' Bunter said, effusively. 'Fellows keep saying that there ought to be another election. Well, I'll do my bit. I'll vote for you, and I'll go canvassing again even though they'll be against you.'

The Bounder's brow darkened for a moment. 'There's not going to be another election,' he said, irritably. 'I'll see to that.'

'Well, I'm your man. I expect you'll need me in the team next Wednesday. I wouldn't turn out for Wharton again, but——'

'You clot!'

'Oh, really, Smithy——'

Sorry, Bunter,' said Smithy, quickly. 'Soccer's rather a sore point at the moment. As you know, Quelch thinks that I tossed that flour from the window the other day——'

'Tee, hee, hee! Jolly good wheeze, that was,' said Bunter, approvingly. 'One up to you, that's what I thought.'

'But I didn't do it,' said Smithy seriously. 'Some rat did it to land me in the soup.'

'Oh?' Like everyone else, Bunter was convinced that Quelch had got the right man, but he wasn't going to say so, not with the prospect of super spreads in front of him. 'Rough luck,' he said, as he concentrated on a box of chocolate creams that Smithy thoughtfully placed in front of him. 'Not bad,' he said indistinctly, cramming half a dozen into his mouth. 'Have one,' he added generously, and pushed the box towards Smithy.

'So there's no soccer for me,' Smithy went on, 'not unless you help me out.'

'Only too pleased.' The fat Owl's fingers dipped into the box again.

The Bounder eyed him narrowly. 'I'd be all right if the bloke who did it owned up.'

'Bet he won't.'

'I don't suppose he will, but Quelch would let me off if someone owned up.'

'Eh? I don't get you.' The Owl sucked the chocolate from his fingers.

The Bounder leaned forward, wondering if he'd prepared the ground well enough. 'I say, Bunter. Why don't you slip that box of chocs into your pocket? I don't need them. You must have seen that there are more in the cupboard. Come to that, I've ordered a tin of toffees, and there's a hamper on its way.'

Bunter's jaw dropped. More chocs, toffees, a hamper! Paradise seemed to be just around the corner. 'Er—I say, Smithy, what were you saying?' he asked, eagerly. 'Did—did you say that I could help you out of a hole?'

Smithy took the plunge. 'You see, Bunter, I'll be all right if someone will own up. Quelch would never find out that the chap who confessed wasn't actually telling the truth.'

'That's right,' agreed Billy Bunter. 'Course he wouldn't. No one wants to be put into extra school for nothing.'

'The person who'd own up for me would have to be a real friend,' said Smithy, slowly.

'You bet,' said Bunter, innocently.

'We're friends, aren't we?'

'Yes,' breathed the contented Owl.

'So why don't you do it?'

'Me?' squeaked Bunter, almost falling off his chair.

'You!'

'But—but I never done it!'

'Of course you didn't, and neither did I. Since Quelch has already got the wrong man, why shouldn't he have another wrong man? It wouldn't make any difference.'

'But—but it would to me.'

'And to me,' said Smithy, quietly.

'Oh, crumbs! I—I say, I—I—honestly, Smithy, I don't care who owns up. It—it can be anyone so long as it ain't me.'

'I thought we were friends,' said Smithy reproachfully. As he got up, pulled a packet of peppermint creams from his jacket pocket, and casually passed them across to the Owl.

Bunter's podgy hands took them automatically, but he continued to gaze at Smithy with startled eyes.

'I—I know, but just think Smithy. It—it would mean being stuck in detention——'

'I don't think it would be as bad as that,' said Smithy, persuasively. 'He'd be easier on you than he's been on me.'

'I dunno about that,' said Bunter, doubtfully.

'He would. He'd think that you'd been really decent if you owned up.'

'Maybe. I suppose he might.'

'Of course he would,' said Smithy, positively. 'I wouldn't be surprised if he let you off altogether.'

'Um!' mumbled Bunter, through a mouthful of peppermint creams.

'It would be quite a joke, pulling Quelch's leg like that.'

'Um!'

'What about it?'

'I dunno.' Unlimited grub was one thing; being stuck in detention was another.

'You'd really be doing me a good turn. I won't forget it, Bunter. I swear I won't. After all, there aren't many blokes who have got the nerve to pull Quelch's leg.'

'True enough,' said the Owl. 'Don't like to boast, but we Bunters don't lack nerve. Never have.'

'What about it?' Smithy asked again.

Bunter shovelled another handful of peppermint creams into his mouth. 'I'll do my best,' he mumbled.

Chapter 22

A Confession

Mr Quelch frowned. 'Bunter!' he rapped.

'Oh!' Billy Bunter had been gazing out of the window, but he jumped to attention at the sound of his form master's voice. 'Yes, sir!'

'Are you listening?'

'Oh! Yes, sir!' I—I heard every word you were saying, sir!'

'Indeed?' Quelch's frown deepened.

It was Tuesday morning, and the form was in the middle of a history lesson. Bunter was inattentive at the best of times, but today he was worse than usual. He blinked anxiously at Quelch from time to time, and two or three times he had opened his mouth and gasped a little, rather like a fish, but then he had closed them again without uttering a word.

Several people had noticed his odd behaviour, and had wondered what the matter was. Toddy had nudged him, and Bob Cherry had given him a friendly hack under the desk to remind him that he was in class, but it had made no difference. However, now that Quelch's gimlet eye was fixed on him, he sat up straighter.

'Since you have been concentrating so hard, Bunter, perhaps you can answer a question.'

'Oh, lor'!'

'What was that, Bunter?'

'Oh! Nothing, sir. I—I——'

'Who led the Norman forces at the battle of Hastings?'

'Smithy, sir!' said Bunter, promptly.

'What?' Quelch's eybrows shot up.

'Oh, oh! I—I didn't mean Smithy, sir!' stammered Bunter. 'I—I mean—what I meant was—oh, crikey!'

Mr Quelch sounded stern. 'Then what did you mean?'

'Um—er—I—I—oh, lor! That is, I didn't mean nothing. Well, you see, I—I—er——'

'Well?' demanded Quelch.

'P—please, sir, I—I—I've got something to tell you,' stuttered Bunter.

'Whatever it is, it can wait until later on. Come to my study after class. I am not having this lesson interrupted by you.'

'I—I—I wanted to say—that is, I—I wanted to say it be—before class started, only——'

'Only what?'

'Only—only I didn't.'

'Upon my word!' Quelch gazed in astonishment at the fattest member of the Remove. 'What have you to say that is so important? Perhaps you had better tell me now.'

'I—I—I—' Bunter dried up. After having had that tea with the Bounder, and with the glorious prospects of many more to come, he had practised his speech to Quelch, and it had seemed surprisingly easy. Now that he had come to make it, it was surprisingly difficult.

'Come along, Bunter,' said Quelch, irritably. 'If you have something to say, say it.'

'Oh, Mr Quelch. I—I—you see, what I mean was—was nothing, sir.'

'Suffering cats!' whispered Bob Cherry.

'Bunter!' The thunder in Quelch's voice rolled round the room. 'It seems to me that you are deliberately wasting time because you cannot answer a simple question. I asked you who led the Norman forces at the battle of Hastings. Answer——'

Bunter's mouth opened, and the words popped out. 'It was me, sir!'

'You!' Quelch was astounded at this extraordinary reply.

'Me! It was me!'

Quelch gazed at him, and so did the rest of the Remove. 'Bunter,' he began.

'It—it—it was me, sir,' repeated Bunter, dismally. 'It was me all the time. I—I want to own up, sir.'

'He's crackers!' murmured Frank Nugent.

'Round the bend,' agreed Johnny.

'That will do!' Mr Quelch glared round the class, and the mutters died away. 'Bunter, you absurd——'

'Oh, really, sir!'

'I want you to explain just what you are talking about, Bunter.'

'I—I—I did it, sir,' mumbled the fat Owl, miserably.

Mr Quelch frowned. 'And what was it that you did?'

Billy Bunter quaked. 'What I mean, sir, is that it was me all the time. I—I—I chucked it——'

'You did what?'

'Like I said, I—I chucked, that is, I—I threw it, sir——'

'What did you throw?'

Bunter opened and shut his mouth several times, and then he swallowed and tried again. 'The bib—bub—bib—bub—bob—' he stuttered. 'I threw the bib—bob—bub—bag, sir.'

Mr Quelch looked completely baffled. 'The bag?' he repeated.

'Yes, sir,' gasped Bunter, relieved that he'd got it out at last. 'I—I—I'm sorry, Mr Quelch. It was me that chucked it—I mean I throwed it—I mean it was me who threw it out of the window. I—I want to own up, sir.'

Mr Quelch's eyebrows shot up again, and chaps swivelled round to look at the fat Owl. The Bounder drew a deep breath, and looked relieved. Skinner and Snoop exchanged amazed glances.

'Upon my word! Am I to understand, you wretched boy, that you are confessing to having thrown that bag of flour out of Vernon-Smith's study window?'

'Oh, lor'!' There was no going back on it now. 'Y—y—yes, sir!'

'I can hardly believe it, Bunter. You are telling me now that you are guilty——'

'Yes. It—it was me——'

'And that you permitted another boy to take the blame so that I punished him unjustly——'

Bunter shook like a blancmange. 'Y—yes, Mr Quelch.

'Upon my word! I hardly know what to say to you.'

'I—I—I——'

'Say no more, Bunter. I shall have to consider how best to deal with you. Come to my study after class!'

'I—I——'

'Be quiet, Bunter!'

There was absolute silence in the form room. No one spoke, but Skinner gazed at Bunter as if thunderstruck. Everybody else looked at the Bounder, feeling rather ashamed of themselves.

'Vernon-Smith,' said Mr Quelch, quietly.

'Yes, sir?'

'It is apparent that I have punished you for an act which you did not commit, and I am sorry about that. I must, however, point out that you only have yourself to blame. You kept that bag of flour for some lawless purpose, and you lied about it when I questioned you. Your detention is cancelled.'

'Thank you, sir,' said the Bounder, politely.

Chapter 23

All Right for Bunter

'I say, you fellows!' began Bunter, as the Remove left the form room.

'So it was you!' exclaimed Johnny Bull.

'Eh? What? Oh—oh, yes. But I say——'

'And you let poor old Smithy take the blame!' said Frank.

'Well, but—but——'

Bob turned to Hurree. 'We did wonder about him. Remember? We found him slouched in the Rag looking like a slug.'

'Oh that's too much, Cherry!' exclaimed Bunter huffily.

Harry Wharton eyed the fat Owl curiously. Although he had thought the Bounder innocent, it hadn't occurred to him that Bunter was guilty, and he had been staggered when the fat man owned up. Owning up wasn't one of his characteristics.

'How did you keep it dark for so long?' Harry asked.

'Er—um—dunno. But I say——'

'I suppose you were decent to confess, but you took your time.'

'De—decent. Was—was it? Oh, oh, of course it was. Couldn't let Smithy take the blame.'

'Just the same, you ought to be kicked,' said Squiff fiercely.

'All over the place,' added Johnny.

'Who? Me?' squeaked Bunter, in alarm.

'Yes, you! Smithy's had a bad time—stuck in detention instead of playing soccer, and all of us thinking that it was his own fault.'

Peter Todd scratched his head. 'What beats me,' he said, 'is how that tub of lard ever had the nerve to chuck flour at Quelch.'

'Dashed if I know,' agreed Bob. 'He wouldn't own up to his own name if he thought it might get him into trouble.'

The crowd grew, and Billy Bunter blinked nervously at them through his big, round specs. 'I—I say, I—I've got to go along to Quelch, and—and——'

'I wouldn't waste time if I were you,' advised Harry.

'Do—do—do you think he'll be mad with me?' asked the Owl. 'Smithy—Smithy said—' He suddenly broke off. 'No, what I meant was——'

'What did Smithy say?' asked Toddy.

'Nun—nun—nothing— He didn't say nothing. I—I haven't spoken to Smithy,' gabbled Bunter, hastily. 'Got—got nothing to say. What I meant was, do you think that Quelch'll go easy on me because I've been decent? Owned up and got Smithy off the hook. Think he'll let me off?'

'I don't think I'd bank on it,' Bob replied. 'You know what masters are like. They're unreasonable. Seem to think it a bit insulting to have bags of flour bursting all over them.'

As the crowd burst into laughter, Vernon-Smith and Redwing came out of the form room. Smithy's face had a faint sarcastic grin, but Redwing's expression was bright now that the Bounder was out of trouble and free to enjoy his new career.

Redwing halted. 'You fat fiend!' he said to Bunter.

'Oh, Redwing! What a beastly thing to say,' protested the Owl.

'You ought to be booted all over the school! It was a lousy thing to do. Smithy's had a bad time because of you.'

'At least he got round to confessing,' said Bob.

'He took his time! You're a rat, Bunter. I ought to punch your head in.' Redwing made a threatening gesture.

The Owl dodged behind Bob Cherry. 'Keep off, you beast!' he hooted. 'Don't you go touching me, Reddy!'

Vernon-Smith grabbed Redwing's arm, and guided him past Billy Bunter. 'Leave him alone, Reddy. It's over. I'm in the clear.'

Redwing swung round to glare at Bunter again. 'Just the same, he deserves a thumping.'

'Forget it,' said Smithy, easily.

'Do you mean that you're going to let that flabby fishcake get away with it?'

'Got it in one,' said Smithy, and he towed his friend out into the quad.

'Beast!' said Bunter. 'He jolly well wouldn't call me names if he knew——'

'You've got trouble enough, fat man,' said Ogilvy. 'You've still got to face Quelch.'

'Oh!' groaned Bunter. 'I—I know, but Smithy

—well, he thought that maybe——'

'Maybe what?'

'Eh?'

'What did Smithy think?' asked Bob, patiently.

'Did—did I say Smithy? No, what I meant to say was that I've been decent. Came straight out. Didn't hesitate for a minute. Don't you think that Quelch might let me off because I've been so straightforward? I—I don't want extra school for the rest of the term. I mean to say, it wouldn't be worth it, would it?'

Bob stared at him. 'What wouldn't be worth it?'

'Oh, oh, nothing!' Bunter said, quickly. 'I—I mean, I owned up because—well, just because I done it.'

'We all know that you did it, fathead,' said Frank.

'Oh, do you? No, yes. Yes, of course you do. I—I wasn't pulling Quelch's leg. Wouldn't do anything like that, not to Quelch. I—I just owned up because it—it was the right thing to do, because I'm decent, that's why. Do—do you think that Quelch might see it that way?'

'You'd better go and find out,' Bob said. 'I can tell you one thing. You won't improve his temper if you keep him waiting.'

'Oh, lor',' mumbled Bunter, and trundled off reluctantly to Quelch's study.

He had done his best for the Bounder, just as he had promised. Smithy was out of trouble, and study no 4 was going to be a land flowing with milk and honey, but that land seemed strangely distant as he tapped at Quelch's door.

'Come in!'

Slowly, the Owl opened the door, and he rolled even more slowly over to Mr Quelch's desk. He looked at his form master, and his fat heart, which had sunk to his shoes, edged up to his ankles. Quelch looked thoughtful rather than furious.

'As I said, Bunter,' began Mr Quelch, 'I have been thinking things over. One of the things that I have taken into account is the fact that you are the most stupid and obtuse boy that I have ever met.'

Bunter goggled at Quelch. 'Oh, sir!' he said. 'Me?'

'You should be punished severely,' Mr Quelch continued, 'but there is one thing in your favour.'

Bunter's heart moved up to his knees. 'Really, sir?'

'Yes. Your confession has prevented an act of injustice to Vernon-Smith.'

'Oh, sir!' breathed the Owl.

'I caned Vernon-Smith, Bunter, but you need not have that on your conscience. He was caned for lying.'

'Shouldn't lie, should you, sir?' said the Owl virtuously.

'The fact that his innocence has been established is due to you.'

By now, Bunter's heart had almost reached its accustomed position. 'Thank you, sir.'

'You made a confession of your own accord, and because of this, I have decided to pardon you.'

'Oh, I say!' gasped Bunter. He could hardly trust his fat ears. 'Oh! M—m—may I—I go now, sir?'

'You may, Bunter.'

Bunter scuttled out, his fat little heart beating away quite happily in the place where it belonged.

Chapter 24
Tit for Tat!

There was a buzz of excited voices coming from the Rag as Harry Wharton approached it. Like everyone else in the Remove, knowing that Smithy was posting the team list for the match against Rookwood, he had come along to see what changes he had made, but as he opened the door of the common room and walked in, heads turned, and the babble of noise stopped.

Puzzled by this extraordinary silence, he looked

around the common room. His friends were standing together. Bob looked red-faced and angry, and the other three had grim expressions on their faces. Mauly was frowning, while Squiff, Toddy, Russell and one or two others looked uncomfortable. The Bounder had a triumphant smile on his lips as Harry stared about him.

Harry walked across to Bob. 'Is the list up?' he asked.

'Yes.' replied Bob, sounding tight-lipped.

'What's wrong?'

'Smithy's been throwing his weight about,' growled Johnny. 'You'd better see for yourself.'

'Oh!' As Harry went across to the notice board, he was aware that everyone was looking at him. He ran his eye down the list. The team was similar to the one he would have selected if he had still been captain, but there was one important difference. Smithy had put himself in Harry's position and had included Redwing. Harry was out of the team.

Everyone was watching, wondering how he would react, and even Billy Bunter managed to struggle into an upright position, and sat in his armchair, blinking through his specs.

Harry stood with his back to the room, trying to control the anger and resentment that he felt. He knew that Smithy regarded it as tit for tat. He had been dropped from Harry's team, and so he was getting his own back, but the circumstances weren't the same. Harry had had some justification, but the Bounder had none. It was just personal enmity.

Actually, Smithy had overstepped the mark. Practically everyone thought that he had gone too far. Harry felt that he could cause the Bounder a great deal of trouble if he chose, but if he did, he would split both the form and the team.

Smithy's look of eager anticipation faded away when no outburst of rage came from Harry. 'Look at him,' he whispered to Redwing. 'He hasn't even got the guts to have a row!'

'You know it isn't that, Smithy. Look here, you know he ought to be in the team.'

'Not likely. I'm enjoying this. All I've done is to turn the tables on him. He kept me out, so I'm doing the same.'

'And you call yourself a sportsman?' muttered Redwing.

'That's right.' The Bounder gave him a mocking smile. 'I'm as much a sportsman as Wharton is.'

Skinner winked at Snoop as Harry returned to his friends. 'What do you think of the team, Wharton?' he called.

Harry didn't bother to turn round. 'It's not at all bad,' he said, coolly.

'I say, Harry,' said Frank, almost choked with indignation. 'You shouldn't stand for it. Smithy's just being vindictive.'

'It's nothing to do with me. Smithy can choose who he likes. He's captain.'

'Don't be a goat!' growled Johnny. 'Everyone's sick of him. Smithy would back down if you spoke out. He'd have to.'

'We'll jolly well make him!' said Bob, savagely. 'You can see what Squiff and Toddy and that lot think——'

'Yes.'

'Well, then,' said Bob, hotly. 'Why should that rotter get away with it? If you're not in the team, then neither am I. Smithy can find another sweeper——'

'And a goalie,' added Johnny.

'And a striker,' said Hurree. 'I do not think that I care to play with someone who is so petty.'

'Most of the team feels the same,' declared Frank. 'They're itching to let him know just what they think of him.'

Harry gave his friends a faint smile. This was the

sort of thing that he had had to put up with when five of the team had marched into his study to inform him that unless he included Smithy in the team, they wouldn't play.

'You can't do that,' he said, quietly. 'It'll destroy the team. Smithy will have to grub around to replace players, and we don't want the Remove to take the same kind of licking that Courtfield gave us, do you? I know that Smithy didn't give two hoots when he put me on the spot, but I do, and I'm pretty sure that you do too.'

There was a moment of silence before Bob said, 'That's rubbish. He'd give in.'

'Would he? I didn't, did I? It's not worth risking.'

'But——'

'Forget it,' said Harry, firmly. 'We've always played the game. We're not going to sink to Smithy's level, are we?'

'Rot!' snorted Johnny.

'It's not the same,' argued Frank. 'He's got no reason to drop you.'

'Frank's right,' said Bob.

'You're bending backwards so much that you're asking to be trampled into the dust,' said Frank.

'And remember, my dear Harry, dust gets blown about by the wind.'

'Okay,' said Harry, calmly. 'So Smithy's behaving like a tornado. Well, that's just too bad. He's the captain, and that's that.'

'I think you're off your head,' growled Johnny.

'All right, so I'm round the bend.' Harry took a last glance at the team list, and he strolled away, knowing that he'd squashed a little rebellion.

Although he hadn't heard what had been said, the Bounder had been watching the faces of the Famous Five. 'It's like I said, Reddy,' he said, with a malicious smile. 'Wharton hasn't got the guts of a tapeworm.'

'That's a bit much,' said Redwing. 'Wharton's

being really decent. He could have stirred up quite a lot of trouble if he'd cared to.'

The Bounder shot an amused glance in the direction of Billy Bunter, who had collapsed back into his armchair now that the excitement was over, and he pointed to him. 'You've got it wrong, Reddy,' he said. 'The decent bloke is that fat porcupine over there,' and he laughed aloud at his friend's puzzled expression.

Chapter 25

Quelch Sees It All

It was a bright autumn afternoon, but Harry Wharton wasn't feeling particularly bright.

'Wharton!' said Mr Quelch, looking at him.

'Yes, Mr Quelch.'

'I see that you are not playing football this afternoon.'

'No, sir.'

'There is nothing wrong with you, is there?' asked Quelch, sounding concerned.

'No, I'm fine, Mr Quelch.'

'But the team is playing Rookwood, I believe?'

'Yes.' Harry could hardly explain to Quelch that Smithy had left him out of the team out of sheer malice, and that because of that, he hadn't cared to be a spectator.

Actually he had decided to go for a cycle ride later on, but when Quelch came across him, he was leaning against a wall, his hands in his pockets, wondering if he could be bothered to go out at all.

Mr Quelch had been taking his accustomed stroll beneath the study windows when he had spotted Harry Wharton hanging about in a rather aimless manner. Quelch, although uninterested in games,

'I SEE THAT YOU ARE NOT PLAYING FOOTBALL THIS
AFTERNOON.'

took his responsibilities very seriously, and he had remembered the important Rookwood fixture. It struck him as strange that one of the best footballers in his form should be in Greyfriars instead of at Rookwood.

Mr Quelch gave Harry a sharp look. He had wondered what had caused an election in the Remove, and he had not been particularly pleased at its outcome. Now, he realised, there must be more trouble, but he asked Harry no further questions, and strolled on.

Harry was feeling depressed. He could imagine the scene at Rookwood, and he knew that Smithy would be playing the game of his life, determined to win. If he did, he would come back trailing clouds of glory.

'Poor old you, Harry!' squeaked a fat voice.

Wharton started as if he had been stung, and he looked up to see a fat figure, a fat face, and a pair of big spectacles that glimmered in the sunlight.

Bunter gave him another sympathetic blink. 'Poor you!'

Harry Wharton breathed hard. 'You soppy scrounger!'

'Oh, really, Wharton!'

'Buzz off!' snapped Harry. He didn't want Bunter's sympathy. He was strongly tempted to help Bunter on his way by planting a foot on the tightest trousers in Greyfriars, but he restrained himself.

Billy Bunter didn't buzz off. He reckoned that Harry was having a tough time so, whether he wanted it or not, he was going to have the Owl's sympathy. 'Nothing to get shirty about, Harry, old man,' he said. 'I just wanted to say that I think it's rotten that you've got to hang about while the others are playing. It's put your nose out of joint, hasn't it?' Harry breathed even harder. 'Keep your chin up, old man. It's no good getting down in the mouth. T'ain't Greyfriars style. Chin up!'

'Clear off!'

'Well, I like that!' said Bunter indignantly. 'I find you looking as if you've lost a box of chocs and found a cough drop, and you can't even be bothered to be civil when I try to cheer you up.'

'Oh, push off!'

Billy Bunter put his grubby hand in his pocket and dragged out a paper bag. 'Have a choc,' he said. 'Won't half make you feel better. Nothing like a choc to cheer you up.'

'No thanks.'

'Go on,' urged Bunter. 'Have one—no, two, if you like. I've still got lots left, and I know where to get more,' and he gave a great, fat chuckle. 'They're the best you can get. Ever known Smithy not to have the best? That's one of the things I like about him.'

Harry shook his head. 'You are a stupid clot, Bunter. If you've been raiding Smithy's study, he'll skin you alive when he gets back from Rookwood.'

'Hee, hee, hee!' chuckled the fat Owl.

Harry looked at him in surprise. Normally, Bunter would have quaked with terror at the idea of the Bounder on the warpath, but he seemed quite unconcerned.

The fat Owl dug his paw into the bag and shoved another three or four chocolates into his cavern of a mouth. He munched appreciatively, managing to smear a great deal of chocolate round his mouth as he did so.

'And you'd better wash before the team gets back. Smithy won't have to be much of a detective to discover who's had his chocolates.'

The fat Owl chuckled again. 'That's all right,' he said. 'Don't you worry. Look here, have some. Go on. They're smashing. I think it was a bit hard, dropping you like that. Still, cheer up! I'll have a word with Smithy. See what I can do. What do you think about that?'

'Nitwit!'

'Well, Smithy's captain, ain't he? The match against St Jim's will be coming off soon and Smithy's going to keep you out, but it would make a difference if I put in a good word for you.' Bunter gave Harry a friendly blink. 'It's tough on you.'

'Roll off, idiot.'

'Now you're getting shirty again,' said Bunter reprovingly. 'It's not my fault you're down and out.' He shoved the bag under Harry's nose again. 'Sure you don't want one. I can jolly well get some more.'

'I told you what will happen when Smithy gets back. I wouldn't risk it if I were you. He'll take you to pieces.'

There were more chuckles. 'Take me apart? Not likely. He wouldn't do that, not what after what I've done for him. Hee, hee, hee! One good turn deserves another, don't it? Crikey, Smithy wouldn't be at Rookwood if I hadn't pulled Quelch's leg for him.'

'What?'

'No, no! Not that. If—if I hadn't owned up,' said Bunter, hastily correcting his mistake. 'I—I—I didn't do nothing like pulling Quelch's leg. No, I owned up because I did it, like I said. Didn't have him on. Wouldn't.'

'Have him on?' repeated Harry, bewildered.

'Nothing of the kind, and Smithy never had anything to do with it. It wasn't him who told me to keep it dark.'

'Oh!' Harry was staggered. It had never occurred to him to doubt the fat Owl's story, but he'd given himself away. 'You bloated buffoon, Bunter! So it was a put-up job, and it was Smithy who put you up to it!'

'No!' gasped Bunter, in dismay. 'Nothing of the sort. Wasn't like that. I say,' he went on, anxiously, 'don't you go saying it was. Quelch might get to hear about it. Be—be—besides, you've got it all wrong. It wasn't Smithy who put me up to it—nothing of the sort. And don't you think that I did it after he gave me a spread in his study, because I wasn't there when we had it. It wasn't Smithy who said it would be a good idea to pull Quelch's leg. He—he never——'

'Shut up!' hissed Harry, as a tall, angular figure turned the corner and came towards them.

Bunter took no notice. 'I tell you he never!' he hooted. 'Never done nothing like that. Don't you go round telling people that Smithy said it would be a joke to pull Quelch's leg. Crumbs! There wouldn't half be a row if Quelch heard about it. He'd be in a rage, that's what he'd be if he knew that Smithy said it would be a good idea if I owned up and got him off the hook. So you——'

'Bunter!'

'Oh, crumbs! Oh, crikey!'

Bunter spun round on his heels, his eyes almost popping through his specs, his mouth open, quivering with terror.

'Bunter!' said Quelch again.

'Oh, lor'!' Bunter quavered.

'I heard every word that you said, Bunter.'

'Oh, hamburgers!'

Quelch looked at him with steely eyes. 'Follow me to my study, Bunter!'

'Oh, acid drops,' said the Owl mournfully.

As Quelch swept back into the House, a disconsolate, fat Owl trailed behind him, and Harry Wharton watched them go, wondering what was going to happen next.

Chapter 26
Ordered Off!

'Bunter!'

'Oh, crikey!' As Bunter stood in front of Quelch, his knees knocked, and he felt that his legs weren't going to be able to support him much longer.

The expression on Quelch's face was positively terrifying. Bunter had often seen Quelch in a temper, and then his brows were knitted in a deep frown and his gimlet eyes glinted, but the fat Owl had never seen him looking as grim as he did now.

'You have deceived me, you wretched boy!'

'Oh, sir!' gasped Bunter. 'No, sir. I—I wouldn't do that, Mr Quelch. I—I—I——'

'You confessed yesterday, Bunter, to having thrown that bag of flour from Vernon-Smith's study.'

'Yes, yes. I—I—I owned up, sir. I—I——'

'Because I believed you. I dealt leniently with you, and now I find that you are unscrupulous, that you have had the audacity to make an utterly unfounded statement enabling another boy to escape a just punishment.'

'But—that is, I—I—I-—,' gabbled Bunter. 'What—what I mean was—I—I—I didn't——'

'What?'

'I—I mean that I—I wasn't. I—I never—you see, it was only a bit of a joke, that's what it was. S—S—Smithy said it—it was a bit of a leg-pull. No, no! Never said nothing, Smithy didn't. Not a word. It was all me. I did it voluntaciously, sir. No, volunteeringly.'

'Bunter!'

'Oh, oh! Cac—can I go now, please, sir?'

'Are you saying that you threw the flour?'

'Oh—er, well, that is, yes, sir.'

'What?' thundered Quelch.

'Oh!' squeaked the Owl. 'No, that's what I meant, Mr Quelch.'

'And so you did not do it, Bunter?'

'Nun—nunno,' groaned the Owl.

'And now perhaps you will tell me just why you made a false confession.'

'I—I—I—' stammered Billy Bunter.

'Well?' Quelch looked piercingly at him.

'It—it—well, you see, I—er—I told Smithy I'd—I'd do my best for him. That's what it was. Oh, crumbs, I wish I hadn't. It—it was only meant to be a but—bit of a joke, sir.'

Mr Quelch stood looking at him. The whole affair was quite clear. Angry though he was with the fat junior, the wretched boy was no longer the main object of his wrath. He could see that Bunter had been nothing more than a catspaw in the unscrupulous hands of Vernon-Smith.

Bunter was one of the most stupid boys he had ever met. He was certainly incapable of planning and carrying out such a scheme. He had been nothing more than a puppet, and Vernon-Smith had pulled the strings.

As Quelch took a deep breath, Billy Bunter gave a nervous blink.

'Bunter!' rapped Quelch.

'Yes, sir?' said the fat Owl, miserably.

'You are a wretched boy!'

'Yes, sir,' agreed Bunter.

'It is quite obvious that you were duped into making a false confession by someone far cleverer than yourself. He took advantage of your obtuseness and almost unbelievable stupidity. I shall take this into consideration .'

'Oh, sir! Thank you, sir!' gasped Bunter. Although he felt that Quelch's description of him was far from accurate, he didn't think it was the moment to object.

His fat face became a little brighter.

'Mum—mum—may I go?' Mr Quelch?'

'You may not,' said Quelch, grimly. 'As I have said, I am aware that you are an incredibly stupid boy, and so your punishment will be less severe than Vernon-Smith's. I shall cane you, Bunter.'

'Oh!' The fat face fell.

'I think, Bunter, that you know what to do.'

'Yes, sir,' quavered Bunter.

Had anyone been listening outside Quelch's study, he would have heard yells and wails as Bunter bent over.

'Yow—ow—ow—ow! Yoo—hoooop!'

A few minutes later, still wailing, the Owl rolled out of the study and wriggled down the masters' corridor.

Inside the room, Mr Quelch put down his cane. His brow grew grimmer as he thought of the Bounder—the wily, wary, arrogant scoundrel who had engineered the whole episode. He had gone off to play in a soccer match, no doubt laughing to himself. He was going to be punished, and he was going to be punished very severely, but until he returned, he was free to enjoy himself, free to do whatever he liked, regardless of the master whom he had fooled and flouted. He was out of reach.

Quelch drummed his fingers on his desk for a minute, and then rose and walked across to the telephone.

Meanwhile, at Rookwood, the Bounder was having a marvellous time. He was playing at the top of his form, and he was backed by a good team. Everything was going his way. Although the team disapproved of what he had done, Redwing was playing better than he had ever played before.

'Stick to it!' shouted Frank Nugent from the sidelines, as Redwing gained possession of the ball, threaded his way between two defenders, and ran on. Smithy raced up the pitch, and Redwing gave him an accurate pass. The Bounder made a lightning dash

. . . AS BUNTER BENT OVER.

towards the goal, and slammed the ball into the net.

'Goal!'

'Well done, Smithy!'

The few Greyfriars supporters leaped in the air with excitement, cheering Smithy's magnificent goal.

The Bounder grinned breathlessly. This was what he had dreamed of, what he had planned for. He was the captain of the Remove, and his rival was back in Greyfriars, aimlessly kicking his heels.

The teams lined up for the remainder of the first half. As the game continued, Mr Dalton, the form master of the Rookwood side, made his way to the pitch. He stood, watching the game, and then he threaded his way through the crowd until he reached a boy wearing a Greyfriars scarf. He tapped him on the shoulder.

'Is a boy called Vernon-Smith playing in your team?' he asked.

'Yes, sir,' replied Frank. 'He's got the ball now.'

Smithy was running down the pitch, weaving his way through the defenders, but then he stumbled. The Rookwood sweeper charged up, collected the ball, and sent it soaring towards the other goal, and Mr Dalton noted the dark scowl that flashed across the Bounder's face.

Although Frank Nugent had turned back, he was looking at the Rookwood master out of the corner of his eye. He had noted his grave expression, and wondered what it had to do with the Bounder. Mr Dalton looked at his watch a couple of times, and then he settled down to wait for the finish of the first half.

By now, the Remove team was on the attack again, threatening the Rookwood goal and hammering in shot after shot, but the goal keeper, who was nearly as good as Johnny, managed to keep the ball out of the net.

As the whistle sounded, Mr Dalton called 'Bulkeley!' to the prefect who was refereeing the match. 'Send Vernon-Smith of Greyfriars over to me.'

The Bounder came off the pitch, quite unable to imagine why a Rookwood master wanted to speak to him.

'Did you want me, sir?' he asked.

'Are you Vernon-Smith?'

'Yes.' The Bounder's manner was almost rude.

'Then I'm afraid you cannot continue to play.'

'What?' Smithy could hardly believe his ears.

'You must leave the pitch.'

As the Bounder stood there, dumbfounded, there were stares and exclamations on all sides.

'What's going on?' asked Bob, as he joined Squiff.

'Dunno. The man must be mad. Why shouldn't he play?'

'He must be crackers!' snorted Johnny.

The members of both teams clustered round Mr Dalton. 'What's wrong, sir?' asked the Rookwood captain. 'We're in the middle of a match.'

'I know. I'm sorry boys, but the headmaster has sent a message saying that Vernon-Smith must drop out.'

Vernon-Smith went red with anger. 'Why should I?' he demanded. 'I'm nothing to do with Rookwood. Your head can't tell me what to do.'

'Calm down, Smithy,' said Redwing, quickly.

'Dr Chisholm has had a telephone call from Greyfriars, Vernon-Smith. You must change and come with me.'

The Bounder's eyes blazed. 'I won't! You can't take me off in the middle of a match. I'm the captain——'

'Don't argue,' hissed Squiff, and he grabbed Smithy's arm.

'Take your hands off me!' The Bounder stared with hostile eyes at Mr Dalton. 'You can't make me leave.'

'What has happened, sir?' asked Redwing. 'Perhaps there's been some mistake——'

'He couldn't have heard right,' said the Bounder, rudely.

'There is no mistake,' said Mr Dalton, coldly. 'I understand that you are playing without permission.'

'That's not true,' said Smithy, quickly. 'I had permission, just like the rest of the team——'

'That's right,' said Bob Cherry.

'It has to be a mistake,' said Redwing again.

'I am afraid not.'

'Then what's it all about?' demanded the Bounder.

'I'll tell you when you've changed,' said Mr Dalton, quietly.

'No! I'm not leaving until you've said.'

Mr Dalton looked at him. 'Very well, Vernon-Smith,' he said. 'It appears that you were put into detention, but you escaped punishment by persuading another boy to confess.'

'Oh, Smithy!' cried Redwing.

The Bounder went white, and then he stared defiantly at Mr Dalton. 'I'll come when the game's over. I'm not leaving now. You can't make me.'

Mr Dalton compressed his lips. 'Go and change immediately!'

'I won't! I'm damned if I will!' The Bounder was wild with rage. His hopes were in ruins. He knew what would happen when he returned to Greyfriars. He would be punished—perhaps even booted out of the school. Since nothing could make it worse, he became even more reckless. 'I won't go! I'm captain of the team, and I'm staying.'

'Smithy, don't!' begged Redwing.

'Don't make a scene!' said Bob.

'You're letting Greyfriars down,' added Johnny.

'Come along, Vernon-Smith,' said Mr Dalton, firmly.

'Not till the match is over!' snapped the Bounder.

'Then there will be no match. The game will not start again until you have left the ground.'

The Bounder gave him a vicious look. He stood there silently, surrounded by players and spectators alike. His own team looked at him in disgust, ashamed of his behaviour, and his head dropped. He kicked at a bit of turf. 'All right,' he muttered.

'As soon as you have changed, two of our prefects will escort you to the station and see you on the train,' said Mr Dalton, as he led the Bounder away.

Chapter 27

For It!

'Smithy!' exclaimed Harry Wharton.

After Billy Bunter had been led away by Quelch, Harry had filled in a rather dreary afternoon by going on his solitary cycle ride. He'd come back in good time for lock-up, not expecting to see any of the team until later. Returning from the cycle shed, he was surprised to see the Bounder surrounded by a small crowd of fellows.

Clearly, Smithy was in a state of smouldering rage, ready to fly off the handle if anyone said a word out of place. Skinner had a sly grin on his face, but the others were only looking curious.

Three or four asked questions, but Smithy elbowed his way through them, tramping silently towards the House. At the sound of Harry's voice, he came to a halt.

'You filthy rotter, Wharton!' he yelled.

Harry looked blankly at the Bounder. Obviously, something had gone wrong at Rookwood, otherwise he wouldn't have been back alone, but Harry couldn't guess what.

'What do you mean? What have I done now?'

The Bounder shot a look of blistering hatred at him. 'Don't act the innocent with me, Wharton. I know perfectly well that you're behind it.'

'Behind what? If you don't tell me what you're on

about, there's nothing I can say.'

'You know what I mean!' snarled Smithy.

'I don't. What's gone wrong? You've come back alone, haven't you?'

'Of course I have,' said Smithy, furiously. 'You fixed it, didn't you? As soon as Quelch heard that Bunter had been lying, he was on the phone to Rookwood.'

'Oh, so that's what it's about,' replied Harry, looking Smithy straight in the eye, 'I hadn't any idea of what Quelch was going to do. How could I? But still, I can't say that I'm surprised. Once he found out that you'd pulled the wool over his eyes, he was bound to do something. I thought he'd just wait until you got back.'

'And how did he know?' The Bounder almost spat the words out. 'You tell me that. Bunter would never have split unless he'd been forced to. He wouldn't have dared. Did you worm it out of him, and then go and bleat to Quelch? Is that it?'

The Bounder stared suspiciously at Harry. Throughout his journey back, he had sat in the train, brooding, convinced that Harry had got the truth out of the Owl, and had then squealed to Quelch.

'It was you, wasn't it?' The Bounder's fists were tightly clenched. 'I know you've been watching and waiting, hoping to get even with me. I know——'

'You know nothing,' said Harry, cuttingly. 'We're not all like you, Vernon-Smith. I didn't dream that you'd got that idiot to confess, and even if I had known, I wouldn't have said a word.'

'Oh, yes? Then how did Quelch——?'

'Because Bunter was babbling to me, and Quelch overheard him. I tried to shut the fat fool up, but he wouldn't listen.'

'Oh!' The Bounder was silent, the wind taken out of his sails.

Harry Wharton shot him a cold look. 'It was just

bad luck that he heard Bunter wittering on. Once he'd got that fool in his study, he'd have had no trouble in getting the story out of him. We all know our Bunter, don't we? But I'll tell you something else, Vernon-Smith. You've been asking for this. You've no one to blame but yourself. Using Bunter was a rotten thing to do. You hit rock bottom when you did that. As it happens, I don't think that you were guilty, but the thought that you twisted that fat fool round your little finger just so that you could get what you wanted makes me sick.'

There was a sharp voice. 'Vernon-Smith!'

The small crowd fell silent as Mr Quelch approached, his face like iron. The Bounder stared at him, and his heart sank.

'I see you are back,' said Quelch, icily.

'Yes, sir,' muttered the Bounder.

'I am taking you to Dr Locke, Vernon-Smith. He will deal with this. Come!'

Silently the Bounder followed his form master into the House. As he watched them disappear inside, Harry Wharton's expression changed.

Although Smithy was wild and reckless, he also had some good qualities. Usually, he was a good sport, capable of great generosity, and he was loyal to his friends. Now, it seemed, Smithy might be sacked from Greyfriars, and infuriating though he was at times, Harry knew that he would be missed.

'Hell's bells!' remarked Bolsover. 'It doesn't sound too good.'

'Poor old Smithy,' said Wibley. 'He might have asked for it, but to be booted out—that's really tough.'

'Out with your hankies,' said Skinner, lightly. 'Let's wipe away our crocodile tears.'

'That's not funny!' snapped Harry.

'Shut up, Skinner!' mumbled Snoop.

Skinner gave Snoop a sharp look, and then he grabbed him by the elbow and led him away before he said a little too much in the hearing of other people.

'I don't suppose there's anything we can do for Smithy,' said Harry, gloomily.

Bolsover shrugged. 'It looks like curtains. I reckon he's had it.'

'But still——'

'I can't make you out,' said Ogilvy. 'Smithy's had it in for you ever since he's been captain. Why should you care about him? His loss is your gain. With him out of the way, you'll be running the show before long.'

'That's nothing to do with it. I honestly think that Smithy's being sacked for something he didn't do. He got that bumbling bladder to confess because he thought his punishment was unjust.'

Harry walked off, still thinking about Smithy.

Chapter 28

Light at Last!

Billy Bunter didn't witness the Bounder's return. For some time after that painful interview in Quelch's study, he'd been in the Rag. He was unable to sit in his favourite armchair, and so he had leaned against a wall of the common room, thinking about absolutely nothing. He didn't even think about food, and he certainly didn't think about Smithy. He just waited until he felt a little more comfortable.

Then, since he was getting bored with his own company, he made his way outside, only to find that other people appeared to be bored with his company too, for they faded away whenever he appeared, and so he made his way towards a massive elm tree close to the wall. He attempted to sit down, but found that he wasn't quite ready for that yet, and so he propped himself up against the trunk of the tree, and

HE PROPPED HIMSELF UP AGAINST THE TRUNK OF
THE TREE . . .

investigated the contents of his sticky pockets, hoping to find a chocolate or two to comfort himself with.

Suddenly he heard the sound of two fellows walking along the path on the other side of the wall, and pricked up his fat ears. They were speaking as they strolled along, and Billy Bunter recognised the voices of Skinner and Snoop.

'You're going too far, Skinner. Smithy's certain to be kicked out. You could see it in Quelch's face.'

'So what?'

'You can't let it happen. It's not fair.'

'Keep your voice down, Snoop.'

'Why? There's nobody about. Look here, Skinner, you've got to do something about it.'

'Why should I?'

'Because Smithy's going to be expelled, that's why. You chucked that bag at Quelch. You should go and say so.'

'Now listen to me,' snarled Skinner. 'You've kept it dark up till now, and you're going to go on keeping it dark.'

Billy Bunter's little round eyes opened wide behind his big, round specs. There was a sticky chocolate in a sticky paw, half way towards a sticky mouth, but in his astonishment, he forgot it, and it remained suspended in the air. 'Oh, crikey!' he breathed.

'You'll keep your mouth shut, Snoop,' Skinner went on, his voice low. 'I only did what Smithy intended to do. He would have done it if Redwing hadn't butted in.'

'That's not the point. You did it, not Smithy. I know he let us down after the election, and he's chucked his weight about. I don't like him any more than you, but I can't stand by and see him kicked out of the school for something he didn't do.'

There was the sound of a slight scuffle. 'Just stay here, Snoop,' Skinner's voice was very unpleasant. 'You're going to keep your mouth shut. Just get it straight. Smithy's being booted out because he got Bunter to own up. It's nothing to do with the bag of flour. Is that clear?'

'Well——'

'What he did was to bribe that fat beanbag to lie for him, and that's what the row is about. It's nothing to do with me.'

'But if Quelch knew that he shouldn't have been in extra school anyway——'

'But he doesn't know, and he isn't going to. Don't try and get away, Snoop. Let's get this settled. You're not giving me away, are you?'

Snoop sighed. 'No, I don't suppose so, Skinner, but I think it's a bit thick.

'He asked for it,' said Skinner, harshly.

'I know, but it all started because of you. It's really a low-down trick. You should go and see Quelch before it's too late.'

'What? Me? Own up?' sneered Skinner. 'Would you, if you were in my place?'

'Yes, I would,' said Snoop, firmly, 'and you should. One word from you——'

'If you can't talk sense, don't say anything.'

'Are you saying that you won't see Quelch?'

'No, and neither are you—' Skinner broke off as he heard a sudden and unexpected exclamation from the other side of the wall.

'Wow!' Billy Bunter's hand flew to his mouth and the chocolate dropped to the ground. He hadn't meant to utter a word. It had just popped out.

Skinner raced up the path, yanked open a small door, and made for the tree on the other side. 'You!' he snapped, as he saw the fat Owl.

'I—I—I say, I—I wasn't listening,' gasped Bunter. 'I—I never heard a word. Did—didn't know that you did it. Never knew you chucked——'

'You were listening——'

The look of fury on Skinner's face made the Owl

back a pace or two. 'Not—not a word. I—I didn't even know you were there, old chap, and—and I never heard Snoop say you buzzed that bag, and—and—' He broke off as Skinner advanced. 'Yaroooo! Keep off! Oh, crikey!'

He fled, in fear of his fat life. Skinner raced after him, hardly knowing what he intended to do. He could punch the fat Owl until his arm ached or he could try to persuade him to keep quiet. There was also the remote possibility that one might lead to the other.

Billy Bunter hurtled out from beneath the trees, and careered across the quad, squeaking with terror as he saw Skinner gaining on him. He nearly stumbled, and then, looking back, gave a wild howl. Then, quite suddenly, he cannoned into someone who was wandering along. 'Ooooh!' he wailed.

'Ouch!' shouted Harry Wharton, staggering as Bunter's bulk crashed into him. He pulled himself together, and snapped, 'What do you think you're doing? Why can't you look where you're going?'

'Keep—keep him off!' yelled Bunter. Breathlessly, he dodged round to the safe side of Harry, and blinked back at Skinner who was still hurtling towards him. 'K—k—keep him off! Don't let him get his hands on me. It—it was Skinner all the time, that's who it was——'

'Who was?' Harry couldn't make out what Bunter was on about.

'Him!' The fat Owl pointed an accusing finger at Skinner who had skidded to a halt. 'Snoop knows it was him. It was him who chucked the flour over Quelch. He bagged the buzz—I mean buzzed the bag out of the window.' As Skinner shot a look of loathing at him, and doubled his fists, Bunter yelled again, 'Keep him off!'

Harry looked from one to the other. 'Stop babbling, Bunter. Start again.'

Fear loosened Bunter's tongue. 'It was him. Snoop knows it was. He don't think it right. It wasn't Smithy at all. It was Skinner. He was the one—chucked it out of Smithy's window. Snoop told him he ought to own up and he said——'

Harry Wharton looked contemptuously at Skinner. 'I see. So you did it, Skinner. I might have guessed. Like the dirty rat you are, you let Smithy take the blame. Quelch will have to know.'

Skinner looked apprehensively at Harry. 'Are you going to tell him?'

'No,' Harry replied, 'but you are. Now that it's out, the news will spread like wildfire. The whole school will know before lights out, and sooner or later, Quelch will hear about it. Your best bet is to go to him before he finds out.'

'Not likely. I don't care what he hears. I shall deny it. There's no proof.' In spite of his words, Skinner looked frightened.

'You might deny it,' said Harry, levelly, 'but if Snoop is asked, I don't suppose he would. Look, Skinner. The game's up. Smithy is with the head now. Go along——'

'You've got a hope!' said Skinner.

'Smithy's for the high jump if you don't.'

'Why should you care? You'd gain if he got sacked.'

Harry ignored this remark. 'Take my advice, Skinner. Go to Dr Locke's——'

'Not on your life.'

'The head might think that there was some excuse for him,' went on Harry, 'if he knew that Smithy had been punished for something that he hadn't done. What about it?'

'Not likely!'

Harry sighed. 'Oh, well, if you won't do it off your own bat, then I'll have to make you,' and he grabbed Skinner.

'You—you—take your hands off me!' yelled

Skinner, but it made no difference. Harry frog-marched him into the House and along the corridor to the head's study where the Bounder was standing, his fate trembling in the balance.

Chapter 29

Beastly for a Man who Did His Best

'I say, you fellows!' Billy Bunter, well aware that the Famous Five were having a particularly good tea, poked his fat head round the study door.

'Slay him!' exclaimed Bob Cherry.

'I—I say, that's going too far, Cherry.'

'Scrag him!' roared Johnny.

'Whaffor?' The fat Owl almost retreated back into the passage, but the sight of the well-spread table was like a magnet.

'Perhaps we should scrag our fat friend first, and then slay him,' suggested Hurree Singh.

'That's not very friendly, Singh,' said Bunter, indignantly. 'What have I done? Only looked in to say——'

'You're a fat villain!' said Frank Nugent.

'Who? Me?'

'And a grasping grunter,' said Johnny.

'Really, Bull!'

'And a mobile dustbin.'

'What's that, Cherry?' said Bunter, looking offended.

'Push off while you're still in one piece,' advised Harry.

'You're a babbling baboon!' shouted Bob. 'We were licked at Rookwood.'

Bunter blinked reproachfully. 'Well, that ain't my fault, is it? I wasn't picked. If Smithy had had me in the team, it would have been different. What with my dribbling and tackling——'

'The score would have been even worse,' said Frank.

'Yah! It's jealousy that keeps me out of the team.'

'Why don't we burst that fat balloon?' demanded Johnny.

'But—but what have I done?'

'If you hadn't lied to Quelch, Smithy would have been in extra school. Harry would have captained the side, and we would have won. Instead of that, Smithy got ordered off—' shouted Bob.

'It—it wasn't my fault,' protested the Owl. 'Quelch shouldn't have listened to me in the quad. Ain't the mark of a gentleman—never thought he was——'

'Well, we would have won——'

'Might have won,' said Harry.

'It was all your fault,' grumbled Johnny.

'And Smithy's,' said Hurree.

'If Smithy isn't booted out——'

'But he ain't,' said Bunter. 'Got let off. He's in his study with Redwing. Jaw, jaw, jaw, that's what they're doing. I was going to drop in, and just happened to hear——'

'What? Through the keyhole?' asked Bob.

'Certainly not, Cherry,' said Bunter, with dignity. 'Couldn't. Smithy's bunged it up with paper. But I couldn't help hearing through a crack in the door——'

'Ha, ha, ha!'

'Smithy got a whacking for getting me to pull Quelch's leg, but he's not going to be sacked.' He edged into the room. 'I say, that cake don't look half bad,' he said, appreciatively. 'Don't think I want any——'

'Good,' said Bob.

'Beast! I—I say, Skinner ain't being sacked either. He got a whacking too, and he's in extra school for the rest of the term. Serve him right, the brute.'

'And how did you hear that?' asked Frank.

'I—I was just going to give him a look in, as a

friend, you know. I hadn't heard that Stott had got a parcel from home or anything like that. Anyway, they slammed the door in my face. Tee, hee, hee! That beast Skinner couldn't sit down. Quelch said that if he stepped out of line again this term, he'd be sacked. Hope he is. He's a rotten beast.' He blinked hopefully at the table. 'I—I say, I've been trudging around. Don't half make a chap hungry.'

'Really?' Bob picked half a loaf, and made a threatening gesture. 'I might let you have this.'

'Eh?' Bunter was baffled. For some reason he didn't seem to be welcome. 'I—I say, do let's be friends,' he said, pathetically. 'I've had a rotten day. Got six of the best from Quelch. I bet his arm was aching when he'd done. Serve him right. I hope he gets plumbago in it. Do you know what he said? He said that I'd lied to him.'

'Did he? I wonder why?'

'Dunno. That's Quelch for you,' said Bunter, bitterly. 'That's him all over. Don't know the meaning of justice, does he? He even put it in my last report. Said I was untruthful. Me! Same as calling me a liar. Can't understand it. The thing is, he's got a down on me. Knows I'm bright. Can't stand competition. Ain't much of a sportsman either, not like me.'

'You are quite right, my dear Bunter,' agreed Hurree Singh, gravely. 'He's not like you.'

'Couldn't be,' said the Owl, complacently. 'He ain't a gent.' His hand rested on the edge of the table, close to a meringue.

'Hands off!' roared Johnny, and the fat Owl hastily put his hands back in his pockets.

'And I had a rotten time with that cad Skinner. Chased me all over the quad. Nearly kicked me. Tee, hee, hee! I'm jolly glad he got it in the neck. Wasn't half glad when Harry marched him off to the head. I bet he would have kicked you. Didn't have the nerve, not with me protecting you.' He looked annoyed at the burst of laughter that followed. 'Can't you lot do any-thing except cackle?'

'Sorry, Bunter,' said Harry, contritely. 'It was good of you to stand up to Skinner for me.'

'That's all right, old man,' said Bunter, generously. 'I don't expect a reward when I lend a hand, but a bit of gratitude makes all the difference. Didn't get a word of thanks from Smithy after all I did for him. I told him I'd do my best, and that's what I did. I pulled Quelch's leg, just like I said. Did it out of friend-ship—because we're pals. Wasn't anything to do with that spread in his study either.'

There was another roar of laughter, and Bunter gave them an indignant blink. 'It's true. He was jolly ungrateful, Smithy was. Do you know what he did when I was outside his study, and he was jawing to Redwing? He chucked a soccer boot at me!'

'Ha, ha, ha!'

The Owl looked mournful. 'And there's Toddy. He's been cutting up rough. He called me names, and he banged my head against the wall——'

'Hard, I hope,' remarked Bob.

'Beast! No, I didn't mean you, Bob, old chap.' The Owl scowled as the Famous Five laughed again. 'I think you might be a bit more pally. Everyone's let me down, but you lot shouldn't. Not after all I've done for you.'

'Like what?' demanded Frank.

'Like giving you tips about soccer. It's your own fault that you lost the match. You could have won if you'd listened to me, especially if I'd been in goal instead of that ass Bull. Anyway, I don't understand it. Everyone's carrying on as if I'm a rotter instead of being the most decent chap in the Remove. I often wonder if it's worth being upright and truthful and loyal when I'm treated like this.'

'It must be a great effort, my dear Bunter.'

'No! Tain't!' declared the Owl. 'Not for a Bunter.

But it gets you down when Quelch makes out that I'm a liar, and Smithy is ungrateful, and Toddy smacks my head, and you lot are too jolly mean to give me anything to eat—' He broke off, as Johnny made his way round the table. 'What—what are you doing, Bull?' He backed towards the door. 'I—I say, Bull, I'm—I'm just leaving——'

'How right you are,' said Johnny, seizing the Owl by the collar, and hustling him out.

There was a wail as Bunter slipped on the floor and skidded before crashing into the wall. 'Yaroooo! Ow! Wow! Wow!'

Bob leaped up and hurled the bread at Bunter. 'Ooooch! Ouch!' hooted Bunter.

'Don't say we haven't given you any grub,' shouted Bob after him. 'If you come back, I'll give you a tin of sardines.'

'Beast!' Billy Bunter didn't take up the offer. Sorrowfully, he rolled away feeling that life was hardly worth living for a really decent chap, especially when he was in a form composed chiefly of beasts.

'Right! Food! said Bob breezily, but they had hardly sat down when Smithy walked in.

Harry Wharton eyed him curiously. Bob frowned, and Johnny Bull snorted. The other two just stared. They were well aware that the Remove was fed up with Smithy. His short time as captain had turned out to be a complete disaster.

Smithy, however, seemed completely at ease as he strolled in. 'Hallo,' he said.

'Sacked?' asked Bob, although he already knew that the Bounder had been let off.

'Nice of you to ask. No.'

'Shame,' grunted Johnny.

Vernon-Smith laughed. 'Thanks again, but don't blame me. Blame Wharton. If he hadn't pushed Skinner into the head's study, I'd be gone by now.'

'He's off his head,' said Johnny.

BOB LEAPED UP AND HURLED THE BREAD AT BUNTER.

'I couldn't agree more. I wouldn't have made the same mistake if I'd been in his shoes.'

'I know,' said Frank.

'Ah, well, we can't all live up to his high standards,' said the Bounder, sarcastically.

'If that's all you came to say,' said Harry, 'you can get out.'

'But that isn't all.' Smithy gave Harry an amused look. 'You really did get me out of a hole, Wharton— more fool you. That rat Skinner wouldn't have cared if I'd been sacked. However, Quelch soon got the truth out of him, so I just got a whacking. Mind you, he made it clear that my character's got the odd black stain or two on it, but I can't say that I'm bothered.' He looked directly at Harry. 'Why did you do it?'

'Why?' repeated Harry, blankly.

'Yes, why? You had me where you wanted me—at least, where I thought you wanted me. I did you down more than once. It was easy to become captain. Because of your obstinacy——'

'Shut up!' snapped Frank.

'But it's true. He knows it's true, and so do I, and so does everyone else come to that. But why didn't you let me stew in my own juice, Wharton?'

'If you don't know, there's not much point in telling you.'

'Mm! Well, perhaps I do know,' said the Bounder. 'Is it a rather old-fashioned virtue called playing the game?'

'Perhaps.'

'You might be surprised, Wharton, to find out that I do know a little something about it.' Smithy became serious. 'I've been pretty rotten, and I'm sorry. I have a lot to thank you for.'

'That's right!' said Johnny.

'There is just one more thing. I've put an official notice on the board in the Rag—as captain, you know.